BLACK HORSE CREEK

Deputy Sheriff Lew Kennett is up against it: the Hap Ivy gang are on the prowl, rustlers are at work, and a thief has been busy in town. When Kennett sets out to capture an outlaw, the situation gets wildly out of hand; and whilst surviving an ambush and preventing a lynching, he is caught up in another facet of local crime and has to kill a townsman. In Black Horse Creek, the sheriff's life is always on the line, and he is determined to beat the odds and stay alive . . .

CORBA SUNMAN

BLACK HORSE CREEK

Complete and Unabridged

LINFORD
Leicester

First published in Great Britain in 2015 by
Robert Hale Limited
London

First Linford Edition
published 2018
by arrangement with
Robert Hale
an imprint of
The Crowood Press
Wiltshire

A catalogue record for this book is available
from the British Library.

ISBN 978–1–4448–3729–2

Published by
F. A. Thorpe (Publishing)
Anstey, Leicestershire

Set by Words & Graphics Ltd.
Anstey, Leicestershire
Printed and bound in Great Britain by
T. J. International Ltd., Padstow, Cornwall

This book is printed on acid-free paper

1

Since dawn Deputy Sheriff Lew Kennett had ridden under a hot and yellow sun which blazed mercilessly in a cloudless, brassy sky. His brown eyes were narrowed against the glare striking up from the hard ground. The law star pinned to his red shirt glinted in the bright noontime. He was sweating profusely, his tall, muscular body tense and stiff from the effort of riding and the stress of anticipating an ambush. He was on the trail of Sim Walton, one of Hap Ivy's gang of bank robbers. Walton had been careless, having shown himself in the cow town of Black Horse Creek the previous night.

Kennett had spotted the outlaw leaving town and followed immediately, hoping for a quick capture. Hap Ivy and his gang had been busy around Fairfax County for some weeks, and

Walton's appearance gave Kennett the suspicion that the local bank was next on the gang's list. Walton seemed to be in no hurry, but was moving as if he had some particular destination in mind. Kennett hoped to find the gang's hideout. Sheriff Dobey in Fairfax, the county seat, had been pushing for results against Ivy and his crooked bunch, and this was the first time Kennett had been lucky enough to latch on to one of the bad men.

The trail led north to the remote area of the county where Kennett would expect to find those men who were shy of the law. He kept glancing at his surroundings, half-expecting an ambush, but the great silence of the illimitable outdoors pressed in around him and he felt as if he were the only human alive in this desolate region.

A rifle slug crackled in his left ear. He dived sideways out of his saddle before the distant report of the shot sounded, and hit the ground hard on his left shoulder. He rolled into a depression, snatched his pistol out of its holster and gripped it with a clammy hand as he listened to the rolling echoes of the shot fading into nothing. He thrust off his hat, cuffed sweat from his forehead, and raised his head slightly to look around. A bullet kicked dust into his eyes. He dropped back into cover as another series of rolling echoes fled to the horizon.

He looked for his horse, saw it had halted twenty yards away from where he was crouching. The butt of his Winchester, protruding from its saddle boot, seemed to mock him. He needed the long gun, but there was too much open ground between him and the horse to make an attempt worthwhile. He raised his head to risk a second glance, saw a large rock six yards to his left, and sprang up to make a low dive towards it.

He slithered behind the rock as a 44.40 rifle slug smacked into it. Sweat ran into his eyes. He gasped for breath. He gripped his pistol, dropped flat to peer around the rock at ground level, and saw nothing but empty country. He was trapped and the ambusher seemed to be holding all the aces. He caught a glimpse of gun smoke drifting along a ridge and realized that it was out of range of his pistol.

He tried to relax behind the rock, his ears strained for unnatural sound. If Walton made the mistake of sneaking into pistol range then there might be an opportunity to turn the tables on him. He knew that Walton was a cold-blooded killer who didn't make many mistakes, but Kennett had always been willing to risk his life for the law badge he wore. Time passed, and he forced his concentration to remain at its highest level.

Kennett risked a look around the rock to get another glimpse of his horse. The animal was grazing on the poor vegetation among the rocks. He called to the animal and it lifted its head, looked in his direction, but did not move. He cursed under his breath, tensed his muscles for a death-defying dash towards the horse, but decided against it. Walton was too good with a rifle and had the edge. There was no percentage in taking reckless action.

Silence stretched out until the waiting became impossible to endure. Kennett risked another glance over the rock, and, when there was no reaction from the outlaw, he sprang to his feet and hurled himself back to the depression he had vacated. Before he was halfway his left leg received a sharp blow, and felt as if it had been struck by lightning. When he tried to put his weight on the leg he fell heavily. He heard the crash of a shot as he fell on his face. He lost his grip on the pistol, snatched it up, and rolled desperately into cover, dropping the gun and reaching with both hands to grasp his left thigh as pain invaded the limb. His fingers slipped on oozing blood. He clenched his teeth, twisted on to his back in the depression, snatched at his neckerchief, and bound it tightly around the painful wound.

He froze when a harsh voice yelled at him. 'Hey, lawman, I got you dead to rights. You ain't got no way outa there and I'm gonna finish you off. Come on out into the open and I'll kill you quick and clean.'

Kennett gritted his teeth against making a reply. He flattened out and lifted his head cautiously, saw gun smoke drifting and ducked as a slug screeched by his right ear. Anger began to boil inside him but he curbed it. He glanced around for better cover, spotted a cluster of rocks to his right, and sprang up and flung himself recklessly at them, ignoring the pain in his thigh. He threw himself flat before reaching cover and rolled desperately to get out of sight before Walton could fire. He made it and lay breathing heavily. A grin appeared on his taut lips as he checked his pistol.

Several shots smacked into his cover, and as the echoes faded he peered out, noting the position of the drifting gun smoke. Walton had come closer. Kennett watched, and saw the crown of a Stetson moving jerkily behind some bushes. He took aim, squeezed off a shot — aiming high to allow for the longer distance — and was gratified to see the hat jerk and disappear quickly. He sprang to his feet and ran for fresh cover, his gun covering the bushes where Walton was crouched.

He gained ten yards before Walton arose from his cover and lifted his Winchester into the aim. Kennett fired two quick shots and went down on his belly. His eyes were squinted against the glare of the sun. He watched Walton intently, saw him jerk and twist before falling awkwardly, and then got to his feet and ran to where the outlaw was sprawled on the ground. Walton had lost his grip on his rifle and was on his back, his eyes closed and his mouth agape. A splotch of blood was widening on the front of his shirt on his right lower ribs.

Walton opened his eyes when he

heard the thud of Kennett's feet on the hard ground, and made a grab for his rifle.

'Touch it and I'll kill you,' Kennett warned, and Walton relaxed.

Kennett moved in. He picked up the discarded Winchester and holstered his pistol. Walton gazed at him, unmoving, his face expressing pain.

'You're Sim Walton, wanted for bank robbery and murder,' Kennett said. 'I'll take you back to Black Horse Creek and jail you. Where's the rest of your gang?'

'You're mistaking me for someone else,' Walton replied. 'I ain't no outlaw. What name did you say? Sim Walton, huh? Hell, I never heard of him. I'm Pete Caswell. I was in Black Horse looking for a riding job. I heard that Circle B might take me on, and I was riding there to talk to the rancher.'

'You're lying. I know who you are. And if you were an honest cowpuncher you wouldn't have ambushed me. I got you dead to rights, Walton, and you're heading for the jail.'

'I'm bleeding bad and like to die before you get me back to town,' Walton said, pressing both hands to the bloodstain on his shirt.

'If you die I'll see you get a decent burial,' Kennett told him.

Walton closed his eyes and relaxed as if becoming unconscious. Kennett checked him over and saw that the bullet wound was not serious. The slug had struck a glancing blow on the lower rib and had been diverted from entering the body.

'You'll live,' Kennett told him. 'I'll patch you up.'

He used Walton's green neckerchief to pad the bullet wound, and then dragged him to his feet.

'Where's your horse?' Kennett demanded.

'It's back of that rise where I lay for you.'

'So why did you ambush me?'

'I saw you following me and spotted your law star.' Walton's mouth pulled into a weak semblance of a grin. 'I never could resist temptation.'

'So you made a mistake.' Kennett pushed Walton to where his own horse was grazing. He mounted and urged the outlaw to head for his own animal.

Walton staggered and stumbled up the slope to the top of the rise, and eventually reached a powerful grey horse that was tethered on the reverse slope. Walton hauled himself into his saddle, swung his mount, and they began the return trip to Black Horse Creek.

★   ★   ★

It was late afternoon when Kennett sighted the cow town, which was sweltering in the slanting rays of the lowering sun. Two rows of buildings faced each other across the wide, dusty main street, deserted at this time of the day. Kennett glanced at his prisoner as they entered the street. They had maintained silence during the long ride. Walton was hunched over his saddle-horn, his eyes closed.

10

'So what were you doing in town last night, Walton?' Kennett demanded.

The outlaw shrugged. 'Just get me into the jail and let me lie down on a bunk,' he pleaded.

The sound of their hoofs echoed as they rode along the street to the jail. Kennett looked around critically, wondering if anything had occurred during his absence. There had been a spate of minor incidents in the past month. Someone had broken into the general store two weeks before, the liveryman had been held up and robbed, and the lawyer's office had been broken into. Abe Wiseman, the attorney, had been stabbed when he investigated a noise in his office. He was still in a dangerous condition in Doc Mitchell's hospital.

There was a sorrel mare standing in the shade of the wide alley beside the law office, and Kennett's harsh expression softened momentarily when he saw it. Sarah Blundell, his fiancée, was in town. He shook his head when he recalled that he was supposed to have ridden over to Fairfax that morning to pick up the engagement ring he had ordered.

He hauled Walton out of his saddle and the wounded outlaw tried a sucker punch in a bid to outwit Kennett, who took the blow on his right shoulder and then cracked his right fist against Walton's jaw. Walton fell into the dust of the street and relaxed. Kennett dragged him up and half-carried him across the sidewalk to the door of the law office.

The door was opened from the inside as Kennett lifted his hand to it, and the slender figure of Sarah Blundell stepped into the opening. She was a tall blonde with blue eyes that seemed to look right through Kennett, and he smiled inwardly. A small flat-crowned Stetson shielded her head and face from the sun. She was wearing faded blue denims and calf-length brown riding boots patterned with tiny white stars.

'At last!' she said quickly. 'Where were you, Lew? I've been waiting ages.

No one knew where you'd gone. You were seen around town last evening, and then suddenly vanished, and your horse was not in the livery barn.' Her voice trailed off when she took in the appearance of Kennett's prisoner, and she gasped at the sight of blood on the outlaw's shirt front.

'I'm sorry you had to wait, Sarah. This is Sim Walton, the outlaw. I spotted him leaving town last night and took out after him.'

'You shot him!' Sarah's face paled under its tan, and then she saw bloodstains on Kennett's left thigh. 'And you've been hurt,' she gasped, her tone filled with sudden concern.

'Perhaps you'll fetch Doc Mitchell,' Kennett suggested, and she nodded and set off at a run across the street.

Kennett pushed Walton into the office. 'Sit down on that chair in front of the desk,' he ordered, and Walton dropped down thankfully, hunching over in pain. Kennett sat on the chair behind the desk. He leaned forward and looked critically at his prisoner. 'You ain't feeling so tough right now, huh?' he demanded.

'I'll be OK after the doctor's seen me and I get some grub lining my insides.'

'Where were you heading when you stopped off to shoot at me?'

'Wouldn't you like to know?' Walton grinned and straightened his shoulders. 'I ain't gonna tell you anything, so why waste your breath? When are you gonna feed me?'

'Wait 'til the doc has looked you over.' Kennett checked the top of the desk, and saw a note that had been written by Thad Cooper, the town marshal, who shared the office and maintained law and order in the town. Cooper had written in his big uneven hand that he'd been told of a sighting of the Hap Ivy gang and had gone to check on the report because he had been unable to find Kennett around town. Kennett shook his head. He was forever telling Cooper to stick to his job in the town and leave county law work to the sheriff's department. But the big town marshal wanted to get into the action.

Doc Mitchell walked in at the door, carrying his medical bag. He was followed by Sarah. The town doctor was short and overweight, aged around fifty. He wore a dark-blue suit with a high collar and a black string tie. His rounded face showed the effect of twenty-five years of flouting the weather in this part of Kansas. He smiled as he approached the desk; a cheerful man who had nursed the sick of the town and the surrounding countryside for longer than he cared to remember.

'So you got back, huh?' Mitchell grinned. He set the bag on the desk and turned his attention to Walton. 'What have we got here?'

'This is Sim Walton, one of the Hap Ivy gang.' Kennett eased his aching leg under the desk. 'He ain't hurt bad. I reckon my leg is worse than his ribs.'

Doc Mitchell checked Walton's wound. 'Nothing to worry about,' he remarked.

'He'll keep for a moment. Let me see your leg, Lew.'

'I'll lock Walton in a cell first.' Kennett got to his feet, biting his lip against a groan as his weight pressed on the leg muscles around his stiffened wound.

Sarah came to the side of the desk, brushing by Walton as she did so, and the outlaw grabbed her left arm and lurched to his feet. He slid his right arm around her neck from behind, cutting off Sarah's cry of shock, and placed the palm of his right hand against the side of her head.

'OK,' he rasped. 'I'm getting out of here, and I'll snap her neck like a dry stick if anyone tries to stop me.'

Kennett drew his pistol in a slick, fluid motion. Three clicks sounded as he cocked the big weapon.

'Let her go,' he rapped. 'You know that won't work. I'd shoot you dead afterwards, and you ain't the type to die for nothing. Turn her loose and I'll put you in a cell so the doc can treat you.

Don't do anything stupid.'

Walton glanced around, his expression showing desperation. Sarah stood motionless in his grip, her eyes wide and fearful, her face ashen in shock. The outlaw paused for interminable moments, and then released his hold and pushed Sarah away.

'Hurry up and get me some grub,' he growled. 'If I wait much longer you won't have to shoot me — I'll die of hunger.'

Kennett picked up a bunch of keys suspended from a hook in the side of the desk. He kept Walton covered with the pistol.

'Sarah, perhaps you'll go along to Allan's Diner and ask him to send in one meal for a prisoner,' he said as he went to a door in the back wall that gave access to the cells. 'Come on, Walton, and don't push your luck again or you won't be breathing when your grub turns up.'

Sarah left the office as Doc Mitchell followed Kennett and Walton into the cell block. The doctor insisted on treating Kennett's wound before checking Walton.

'You've been lucky, Lew,' Mitchell observed as he cleansed and then bandaged Kennett's thigh. 'You should keep your full weight off the leg for a few days, but knowing you I'd say that advice will be ignored.'

Kennett smiled and sat on a bunk in an adjoining cell while Walton's wound was treated.

'He'll live,' Mitchell pronounced when he emerged from the cell. He took the bunch of keys from Kennett's hand and locked the cell door on Walton. 'Just remember to rest up when you can, Lew.'

Kennett pushed himself to his feet and took the cell keys. 'Thanks, Doc. You know where to send your bill. Has anything happened around town since last evening?'

'I heard that Jake Blundell lost some stock yesterday — ten head. He's up in arms about it, and most of his outfit are out looking for the rustlers. I guess that's why Sarah is in town today. Jake probably told her to chase you up.'

Kennett heaved a sigh. He didn't like Sarah's uncle, who had managed the Circle B since his brother Chuck, Sarah's father, had died in a stampede five years earlier. Kennett had enough on his plate without Jake chasing after him every time the wind blew. His life these days consisted of keeping an eye open for Hap Ivy and his gang or chasing around the range after a bunch of rustlers who were operating in a small way, stealing just a few head of cattle here and there. The losses were minimal, and Kennett would rather have had a big loss to contend with. These pinprick raids were not normal, and he was at a loss wondering who was taking big risks for such little gain. Then there were the petty robberies being committed around town. They were not much more than a nuisance, and, somewhere, a small-minded criminal was laughing up his sleeve at the way he was giving the local law the runaround.

'It's the same old stuff,' Kennett said. 'I'll catch up with the crooks one of these days.'

'You want to pray that the bad men won't get more ambitious,' Doc Mitchell observed. 'I'll be seeing you, Lew.'

Kennett followed the doctor into the office and sat down behind the paper-strewn desk. Mitchell departed, and held the street door open for Sarah, who entered the office. She had recovered from her shock of being handled by Walton, but when she approached the desk, her face was expressing concern.

'Are you OK, Lew?' she demanded, standing over him.

He looked up at her and nodded. 'I'm fine,' he replied. 'What brings you into town in the middle of the week?'

'I knew you were going to ride over to Fairfax today and I thought it would be nice to accompany you.' She sat down on a corner of the desk.

'I'm sorry about the change in plans.' He spoke huskily. 'When I spotted Walton on the street last evening I had to follow him, hoping to come up with the rest of the gang. But what happened out at Circle B yesterday? Doc told me you lost some cattle.'

'About ten prime beeves were stolen off the home range out of a herd of fifty.' Sarah shook her head as she considered. 'Doesn't it strike you as odd that the thieves left forty steers and ran off with just ten? What kind of rustlers are they?'

'I've been wondering about that,' he confessed. 'It's happened before. Joe Cantwell lost just eight steers last month, and the same thing happened to Pete Farrell a few weeks before that.'

'The thieves aren't regular rustlers.' Sarah shook her head confidently. 'I suspect it's the work of those nesters over by Moose Jaw Bend. It looks like they're stealing for food. It might pay you to look around there, Lew.'

'I'll chase it up,' he promised. 'I don't

need Jake breathing down my neck about his cattle losses. I'll ride out your way when Thad gets back. He left a note saying he had a tip that Hap Ivy was seen. I wish Thad would leave the out-of-town work to me. But you know him! He's not content with being the town marshal. He'd willingly swap places with me if I'd go along with it.'

'I saw Thad at a distance as I was coming from the ranch,' Sarah mused. 'He was heading towards the Morrison ranch, and looked like he was following a trail.'

'He can't be trailing the gang.' Kennett paused and considered. 'Why would they be riding in that direction?'

'They must be hiding out somewhere on the range.' Sarah looked into Kennett's eyes, and she seemed ill at ease.

'You look as if there's something bothering you,' he observed. 'What is it, Sarah?'

'I think there's trouble building up around here,' she said slowly, as if considering each word before she spoke. 'There's rustling out on the range, and it's growing. You've got trouble here in town. It isn't much yet, but it seems to be spreading; and the violence around here is worse than it was a year ago. It's getting so a woman daren't walk along the street after dark, especially on a Saturday night. Haven't you noticed the difference, Lew? You must have, because you're in the thick of it all the time.'

'I sure have.' He nodded. 'And I'm worried about it. I'm on my own here, and I'm responsible for what happens on the range as well as around town. I know Thad does a good job keeping law and order inside town limits, but he can only do so much. I don't mind admitting that I am concerned about the situation. When I ride into Fairfax to get your ring I'll have a word with Sheriff Dobey about it. I reckon I could do with another deputy here for a spell. It's getting so I don't have any time off duty.'

Sarah nodded. 'You don't have to tell me that. I can't remember the last time we sat on my porch of an evening to watch the sun go down. You used to have a lot of free time, but I hardly ever see you these days.'

'I have been giving your ranch a miss lately.' Kennett suppressed a sigh. 'It's got nothing to do with you,' he added quickly. 'I don't know what's got into Jake, but he seems to have changed. He looks like a man with a lot on his mind. Has he said anything to you about trouble, Sarah?'

'He always rants a lot. I've had a sneaking feeling he thinks the ranch should belong to him. He's only running it for me because I don't know much about the cattle business.'

'I always thought he owned half of it in partnership with your father, and that you inherited your father's share when he died.'

'No. Jake never put a red cent into the business. It was my father's money, and Jake is running the place for me.

We never saw Jake from one year to another when Dad was alive.'

The street door opened at that moment and Kennett swung round to see two rough-looking men with guns in their hands entering the office. He recognized the foremost instantly — a short, stocky man with bandy legs. It was Hap Ivy, the outlaw, and the pistol in his hand looked as big as a cannon.

'Just stand still and don't do anything with your hands, Deputy,' Ivy advised, grinning, although his dark eyes were as cold as ice and just as chilling. 'All I want is Sim Walton, and there'll be no trouble unless you start it. So get your hands up, mister.'

Kennett raised his hands, his pent-up breath escaping in a long sigh as he looked down the barrel of the outlaw's gun.

'You won't get away with this,' he said sharply.

'You just watch me,' Ivy retorted. 'Fetch Walton out here. I'll take this gal with me when we leave, and turn her loose once we're clear of town.'

Kennett remained silent, aware that he had no chance of reacting against this set-up. But he didn't like it, and vowed that one day soon he would make Hap Ivy eat crow . . .

2

Kennett remained motionless until Ivy had disarmed him, and then turned and picked up his cell keys. He led the way into the cell block and Ivy followed him. The other outlaw remained in the office with Sarah. Walton came to the door of his cell when he saw Ivy, and grinned as the cell door was unlocked.

'Gimme a gun,' he snarled as he emerged from the cell, 'and I'll put a slug through this guy.' He pushed Kennett aside. 'He plugged me, and I owe him one.'

'Hold your horses,' Ivy rapped. 'There'll be no shooting in town. I wanta get away nice and easy. Your horse is outside, so go crawl into your saddle and head out with Swig back to the hideout. We'll follow in a few minutes.'

Walton glared at Kennett and went

into the front office. Ivy motioned with his gun.

'Go back to your desk, Deputy, and sit down,' he ordered. 'You know what to do if you wanta stay alive.'

Kennett went into the office and dropped into his seat behind the desk. Sarah was standing in front of the desk, gazing at the other outlaw. She transferred her gaze to Kennett as he sat down.

'Are you gonna let them get away with this, Lew?' she demanded.

'What do you suggest?' he responded. 'They're holding the guns.'

'You've got more sense than the gal,' Ivy observed. 'Now listen to me. When we leave, you'll sit here for thirty minutes before raising a ruckus. When I'm ready to turn the gal loose I don't want to see sign of anyone riding my back trail. You do nothing until she rides back into town. Have you got that?'

'I hear you,' Kennett replied. He watched Walton depart from the office, and told himself that there would be another time and place. Moments later the sound of departing hoofs outside indicated that his prisoner was leaving town.

'I'm disappointed in you, Lew,' Sarah said, disgust lacing her tone. 'You're just standing there while these outlaws ride roughshod over you.'

Hap Ivy laughed. 'Don't be too hard on him, gal,' he said. 'In a situation like this the only thing he can do is get killed, and he knows it. So let it ride. You need to think of yourself. Don't give me any trouble when we ride out or you could find yourself in more trouble than you can handle. Do you get my drift? You're riding with us until we're in the clear, so shut up and stay clammed until I send you back here.'

Sarah opened her mouth to argue but Kennett spoke first.

'Just do like he says, Sarah, and come straight back here when he turns you loose.'

Hap Ivy laughed raucously. Sarah

closed her mouth and compressed her lips.

'Have you got a horse?' Ivy demanded.

Sarah walked to the side window overlooking the alley and pointed to her sorrel.

'It's out there,' she said.

'Fetch it round to the door, Swig,' Ivy said to his silent companion. Kennett looked at the other outlaw and recognized him as Swig Rafferty, bank robber and killer.

Rafferty departed and Ivy waggled his pistol threateningly in Kennett's direction.

'Remember my warning,' he said. 'We're leaving now. Come on, gal.'

Kennett remained in his seat as Ivy ushered Sarah out of the office. He pushed his Stetson to the back of his head and cuffed sweat from his forehead. When he heard horses moving away from the front of the office he got to his feet and crossed to the big window overlooking the street, and was in time to see Sarah riding off between the two outlaws.

He heaved a sigh and retrieved his pistol from the corner where Ivy had tossed it. He experienced an impulse to rush out to the street and shoot at the bad men but resisted the temptation and returned to his desk, aware that he could not expose Sarah to danger. There would be time to take out after the gang when she was back safely in town.

Footsteps sounded on the sidewalk outside the office and Kennett tensed. He dropped his right hand to the butt of his holstered pistol and watched the street door, which opened slowly. He grimaced when Ben Overman, owner of the general store, stuck his head around the door. Overman was a tall, lean man in his mid-fifties. His face was pale, as if he never went out in the sunlight. He was wearing brown pants, a white apron over a grey shirt and a black string tie around his scrawny neck.

'Huh, so you're back at last.' Overman came into the office with a slightly ungainly stride, favouring his right leg. He lost the leg in the Civil War, and had accustomed himself to walking on the wooden limb that replaced it. 'I had a visitor last night, Lew, and as far as I can make out he stole two guns and several boxes of cartridges. And that ain't all. He took provisions and about fifty dollars outa the till. Where you been? I was here at sun-up but there was no sign of you, and I came back several times during the morning. It ain't good enough, you know. What's happening to the law around here? Thad Cooper wasn't around either. Noah Leake at the livery barn told me Cooper rode out before first light, and he's the one we pay to take care of the town against thieves and bad men.'

'Thad shoulda been here,' Kennett said. 'I was on the trail of Hap Ivy's bunch.'

'Did you have any luck?'

Kennett explained what had happened and Overman snorted derisively. 'That's the helluva note!' he exclaimed.

'There's something wrong with your law-dealing if a bunch of crooks can come riding in here in the daytime and spring one of their own outa the jail. What's Sheriff Dobey gonna say about that when you tell him?'

'I'm hoping he'll agree with me that we need an extra deputy in here for a spell,' Kennett replied. 'How did the thief enter your place, Ben?'

'He took a pane of glass outa the back door and used the key I forgot to remove when I locked up. I found the tracks of a horse out back, so you might be able to run him down, although most of a day has been wasted. I'm gonna complain to the sheriff, Lew. I ain't happy about this. It ain't the first time I've been robbed, and nothing has ever been done about it.'

'I'm doing the best I can,' Kennett countered. 'Leave it with me and I'll come and take a look at those tracks soon as I can.'

'You ain't doing anything right now,' Overman observed.

'I'm waiting for Sarah to ride back into town and then I'm heading out after four outlaws,' Kennett said heavily. 'So do me a favour and go tell Art Gemmell to get the regular posse together and follow me to the south as soon as he can. Gemmell can follow tracks, and I might need gun help if I do catch up with Ivy and his bunch.'

'You'd be a whole lot better off chasing after the troublemakers around town,' Overman said, shaking his head.

He departed, slamming the street door behind him. Kennett heaved a sigh. Tense minutes passed, and it seemed like hours before he heard a rider approaching the office. He got to his feet, went to the window, and a sigh of relief gusted through him when he saw Sarah dismounting outside. He opened the street door and she hurried into the office.

'Are you OK?' he demanded.

'I'm angry,' she responded sharply. 'Why didn't you do something about those bad men while they were here?

And what do you think Uncle Jake will say when I tell him what happened?'

'If you're worried about his reaction then don't tell him,' Kennett replied. 'And you know there was nothing I could do. Ivy had me cold, and would have killed me if I'd tried to resist. I played the situation the only way I could. But now you're safe I can ride out and try to pick up the gang, and this time I'll have a gun in my hand. Which way did they head when you left them?'

'I didn't look.' She sounded disgruntled. 'All I wanted to do was get back here.'

'You'd better go back to the ranch and stay there while these bad men are on the loose. I'll ride out to Circle B tomorrow. Right now I've got a score to settle with Hap Ivy.'

Sarah went out to her horse, swung into the saddle, and rode off along the street without looking back. Kennett watched her go, shaking his head, and then mounted his horse and headed out of town in the direction the outlaws had taken, studying the ground for a trail to follow.

He found the spot where the riders had halted when they turned Sarah loose, counted four sets of tracks heading south-east, and dismounted to examine them more closely in order to identify them later. He found some distinguishing marks in the hoof prints and mentally noted them before setting out to follow. After some distance the tracks left the main trail and swung off across the range.

Kennett rode steadily in pursuit. He was furious with himself for having been surprised by the outlaws, and pushed his horse into greater effort in an attempt to gain on his quarry, but the bad men were well mounted, and aware that he would pursue them as soon as Sarah was out of their clutches. When he eventually spotted them in the distance, they were riding over the crest of a ridge ahead, and he felt a tingle of anticipation as he continued, knowing that he was asking for trouble in the form of an ambush. But he kept riding, his nerves jumping as he approached the crest. A sigh of relief escaped him when he gained the top and saw the fugitives riding fast for yet another ridge.

He settled down to a long ride, aware that Ivy would not permit him to follow very far. He wondered where the outlaws were hiding out, and realized that if they were taking refuge on one of the ranches in the county then he would have little chance of catching up with them. A sudden spate of shooting startled him, and for a moment he fancied he was the target. But the shots were not fired in his direction and he spurred for the nearest high ground. He topped a rise and reined in quickly, for two riders were motionless in the middle distance, and gun smoke was drifting from the knot of four riders who were galloping off into the west.

One of the two riders and his horse were down. The second man was standing with his mount between him and the departing outlaws, shooting at the bad men from across his saddle. Dust spurts marked his shots where they were striking the ground, and, although they were close to Ivy and his bunch, none of the shooting was effective. The four outlaws disappeared from sight beyond a rise and the shooting dwindled away, leaving echoes grumbling across the desolate range.

Kennett rode fast to where the shooting had taken place, and the rider still on his feet swung round at the sound of hoof beats. His rifle lifted quickly to cover Kennett, and then dropped when he saw the law star on Kennett's shirt front. Kennett reined in quickly. His keen gaze had already taken in the fallen horse and rider, and a cold chill stabbed through him when he recognized Thad Cooper, the town marshal. Cooper's shirt front was drenched in blood. Kennett slid out of his saddle, trailed his reins, and dropped to his knees beside the stricken lawman.

A glance was sufficient to see that Cooper was dead. He had been shot through the heart. Kennett got to his feet, his mind blanked by shock. He gazed at the motionless stranger, who was watching him. The man was dressed in range clothes, and he was wearing twin pistols on crossed cartridge belts around his waist. He had on a blue shirt and a black leather vest. Dark hair showed where his Stetson had been pushed back from his forehead. His eyes were dark, and his long face was deeply tanned. He gazed at Kennett, his features harshly set.

'Who are you?' Kennett demanded. 'What happened here?'

'I met up with Thad and we were talking when four men came over the ridge back there and started shooting without warning. Did you see them?'

'I'm following them — Hap Ivy and his crooked bunch. How'd you come to meet Cooper out here, and where did you come from?'

'I'll answer your questions later. I'm

Lin Cooper, Thad's brother. He's dead, so let's get to riding and run down those killers. I got a score to settle with them.'

'There'll be a posse coming out from town shortly.' Kennett swung into his saddle. He touched spurs to his mount and the animal set off at a gallop in the direction taken by the outlaws.

Lin Cooper jumped into his saddle and caught up with Kennett within a few yards. He was mounted on a powerful dun stallion, and, giving the animal its head, he forged ahead and rode recklessly after the fleeing outlaws. Kennett ranged alongside him, and they concentrated on getting the best out of their mounts.

The noise of pounding hoofs and creaking saddle leather surrounded them. They reached the ridge where Ivy and his men had disappeared, and Kennett pulled his horse to a halt, for the four outlaws had halted about two hundred yards ahead and were surrounding a wagon that was apparently heading for Black Horse Creek. A man and a woman were on the driving seat of the wagon, and Kennett recognized Rex Morrison of Box M and his wife Aggie.

'What are you stopping for?' Lin Cooper demanded. 'We've got 'em cold now.'

'That's the Box M rancher and his wife on that wagon and Ivy will use them as hostages against us.' Kennett spoke through gritted teeth, thinking of Sarah back in town. 'I don't want to get caught up in that situation so let's stay out of range and see what happens.'

'We can handle them,' Cooper said harshly. 'Let's rush them. I'll handle three of them and you can take care of the fourth.'

'Not if it means dragging innocent folks into it,' Kennett said flatly. His tone stopped Cooper, who let his shoulders sag.

'I guess you're right,' he said reluctantly. 'Let's get back over the ridge and wait for them to ride on.'

Kennett led the way back over the

crest they had just crossed and Cooper joined him. They dismounted, both taking their rifles from their saddle holsters. Kennett trailed his reins and dropped flat to edge forward until he could look down the reverse slope. His eyes turned bleak when he saw Swig Rafferty lifting Mrs Morrison, a woman of around forty, on to his horse behind the saddle. The next moment the outlaws were continuing on their way, taking Mrs Morrison with them. Rex Morrison sat on his wagon, gazing after the outlaws and his departing wife.

When Ivy and his men had disappeared, Kennett remounted and set off towards the wagon. Cooper came to his side, and moments later they reined up in front of Rex Morrison. The Box M rancher was in his fifties, grey-haired and fleshy. His face was pale with concern for his wife, and he gazed at Kennett with disbelief in his dark eyes.

'Outlaws,' Morrison said. 'That was Hap Ivy and his bunch. They took my Aggie — said to warn you to go back to town or I'll never see her again. You've been after those killers for weeks, Lew, so how come they're riding the range in broad daylight like honest men?'

'We've got their measure,' Cooper cut in. 'They won't harm your wife. They'll turn her loose after a couple of miles.'

'A posse will be along shortly, Rex,' Kennett said. 'You go on to town. You'll find Thad Cooper's body on the trail a few miles back. Take it with you. We'll bring Aggie along.'

'Did they kill Thad?' Morrison clenched his hands. 'Heck, they won't think twice about harming Aggie if you tread on their heels. Stay away from them, Lew, for God's sake! I don't want anything bad happening to my wife.'

'I'll do what's got to be done,' Kennett said tensely. 'Get moving, Rex. Aggie will be OK.'

Cooper was already pushing his horse in the direction taken by the outlaws. Kennett motioned for Morrison to get started for town, and, after some hesitation, the rancher cracked his whip and his team threw their weight into their collars. The wagon rumbled on its way, wheels grating and dust flying.

Kennett was angry as he went after Cooper. First Sarah had been used by the outlaws, and now Mrs Morrison. He caught up with Cooper and urged the man to slow his pace. They continued for a couple of miles, and then, crossing another ridge, both men reined in swiftly, for Mrs Morrison was stumbling along towards them, and there was no sign of the outlaws. Relief filled Kennett as he dismounted beside the woman, and she dropped to her knees when she recognized him.

'Are you OK, Mrs Morrison?' Kennett demanded.

'They dropped me off and rode south,' she replied, struggling to her feet. 'Where's Rex?'

'I sent him on to town,' Kennett said. 'I told him I'd take you there. Get up behind me and we'll start back.'

'What about the outlaws?' Cooper demanded.

Kennett shook his head. 'I'm heading back to town. There'll be a posse out by now, heading this way. I'll send them on to look for Ivy and his bunch.'

'I'm going on.' Cooper turned his horse. 'See you in town later.'

'I'll warn the posse you're behind Ivy. Just follow the gang, find their hideout; the posse will close in and take them.'

Cooper shook his head and set in his spurs. He left a cloud of dust behind as he rode out. Kennett watched him, and then turned to help Mrs Morrison up behind him. She clung to him as they set off back to town, and three miles along the trail Kennett saw a group of riders approaching, led by the big figure of the town blacksmith, Art Gemmell.

Gemmell was a tall, powerful man; four inches over six feet in height and superbly muscled. He never wore anything but a sleeveless leather vest on his upper torso, showing off his brawny arms. He held up a massive hand to halt the posse when they came up, and leaned forward in his saddle to rest an

45

elbow on his saddle-horn.

'This is a bad business, Lew.' Gemmell's voice sounded as if it originated in his boots. 'Thad Cooper dead and those outlaws took Mrs Morrison! Glad to see you've got her back. You better hurry on to town because there's more trouble for you to handle. Jake Blundell rode in with some of his outfit. They had young Joe Allen hogtied — said they found him on Circle B grass looking like he was gonna steal some steers, and he shot one of the punchers when they grabbed him.'

'Are you kidding?' Kennett demanded. 'Joe Allen doesn't know one end of a steer from the other, and he sure wouldn't shoot anyone.'

'I'm only telling you what I saw and heard.' Gemmell shrugged. 'Jake reckoned to string up Allen on Main Street, but your gal Sarah calmed him down, and they locked Allen in a cell with a couple of Circle B riders watching the place.'

Kennett explained about Lin Cooper,

and Gemmell rode on with his half-dozen posse men. Kennett continued to town. He passed Rex Morrison and his wagon without stopping, although Morrison shouted and signalled for him to halt when he passed. But Kennett was anxious to get back to town to check on the trouble awaiting him there, and he was relieved when he finally entered the main street.

A restless crowd was standing outside the law office, and a dozen voices began talking at once when Kennett approached. Willing hands helped Mrs Morrison down from behind Kennett and he swung out of his saddle. The law-office door was wide open, and two cowpunchers were standing in the doorway, watching the crowd. They were holding drawn pistols.

'What's going on?' Kennett demanded, pushing through the crowd to gain the sidewalk.

'Those Circle B riders are threatening to lynch Joe Allen,' said Frank Fallon, the hotel owner. A tall, lean man, who was the town mayor and a leading light in the community, Fallon was smartly dressed in a town suit.

'No one is gonna string up anyone,' Kennett said. He went forward and the two punchers backed out of the doorway. He followed them into the office and slammed the door to shut out the noise of the crowd. 'What gives?' he demanded.

'We caught ourselves a rustler on Circle B grass,' said Mort Downey, the Circle B ramrod.

'I heard about it. Do you reckon Joe Allen is a rustler? Hell, he never leaves town. He spends all his time helping his mother run her diner. I don't reckon he would know what beef on the hoof looks like. And you must have better things to do than hang around town.'

'I've got my orders.' Downey was tall, tough, and generally of a sullen nature. 'Allen shot Blint Murphy when Murphy tried to grab him. The doc says Murphy is in a bad way. If Murphy dies there's gonna be a hanging on Main Street.'

'I give the orders around here,' Kennett rasped, 'and you can cut out the talk about lynching.'

'You weren't here when we brought Allen in.' Downey spoke with ill-concealed impatience. 'Jake told me to stick around until you showed up.'

'Well, I'm back now so get the hell out and head on back to Circle B. I can do without your interference. What are you trying to do, start a riot? Heck, I've got enough trouble on my plate without you joining in.'

'Jake ain't pleased with you.' Downey grinned sourly. 'Sarah told him what happened to her when those outlaws showed up, and he is madder than a wet hen. I ain't going back to the ranch. I'm sticking around until I know that Murphy is out of the woods. So don't tell me what to do.'

'Then keep your trap shut,' Kennett rapped. 'Now get outa here and stop giving me trouble.'

Downey opened his mouth to make a smart reply but the expression on

Kennett's face deterred him and he jerked open the street door and departed, followed by Pete Goymer, who grimaced as he caught Kennett's eye. Kennett picked up the cell keys and went through to the cell block. Joe Allen, aged eighteen, was sitting on a bunk in the nearest cell, his elbows on his knees and his head in his hands. He looked up at Kennett's entrance, and jumped to his feet and came to the door of the cell.

'I didn't do anything, Lew,' he said in a high-pitched tone. 'I wasn't stealing cattle, and I didn't shoot that cowboy. I don't have a gun. Mom wouldn't let me touch one.'

'OK, Joe, Settle down and take it easy. Just tell me what happened. What were you doing on Circle B range anyway?'

'Mom gave me the day off from the diner and hired me a horse from Mr Leake. She told me to ride out to Circle B and ask Sarah Blundell for the material to make a dress from.' Allen was tall and robust, a powerful youngster who generally kept himself to himself. He was quiet-natured, worked all hours for his mother in the town diner, and did not gamble or drink alcohol.

'So what happened?' Kennett was wondering if the Circle B crew had been joshing Joe and their rough play had got out of hand.

'A bunch of cowboys showed up before I got to the ranch and they made fun of me. They said I was out there rustling cattle, and Murphy got off his horse and dragged me out of the saddle. He took out his gun and I grabbed his wrist. I thought he was gonna shoot me! The gun went off and Murphy fell down, bleeding. I didn't do anything, Lew. It was an accident. But Mort Downey said the gun was mine and I shot Murphy deliberately. He said I'd be hanged if Murphy died.'

'Was Jake Blundell with his crew when Murphy was shot?' Kennett asked.

'No. He came up afterwards. He said for me to be brought to jail. Can I see my mom?'

'Sure, Joe. Just settle down and relax. I'll get your mother here soon as I can.'

A gun crashed outside on the street. Kennett turned instantly and ran through the office to the front door. The gun fired again, hammering out the silence. Kennett clenched his teeth and jerked the door open. He hastened out to the sidewalk, and pulled up short when a gun muzzle was thrust violently into his stomach.

3

Mort Downey confronted Kennett, his gun muzzle jabbing painfully into Kennett's belly. Pete Goymer was wrestling with a townsman. Downey thrust his gun hand forward, digging his muzzle harder into Kennett's stomach.

'Keep out of this,' Downey snarled. 'It's a private thing.'

Kennett twisted sideways and his left hand swept in to thrust against Downey's gun wrist, knocking the pistol aside. He secured a grip on the wrist and thrust Downey's arm away, simultaneously clenching his right fist and smashing his hard knuckles against Downey's chin. Downey went over backwards, his feet scrabbling on the sidewalk. He collided with three townsmen and they all fell off the sidewalk into the street. Kennett drew his pistol and cocked it.

Downey came up off the ground like

a cat, his right hand sliding around his waist to his spine, reappearing a split second later filled with a small-calibre pocket gun. When Kennett spotted the weapon he squeezed his trigger. The crash of the shot thundered around the street, hurling echoes far and wide. Downey took the slug in his right shoulder, dropped his gun, and then followed it down into the dust.

Most of the townsmen froze at the sound of the shot, but Goymer now had his opponent around the neck with his left arm and was punching relentlessly with his right fist, battering the unfortunate townsman's face. Kennett stepped forward and slammed his gun barrel against Goymer's right temple. The Circle B cowpuncher dropped to his knees as if he had been poleaxed, and then pitched forward on to his face and relaxed.

'What in hell is going on?' Kennett demanded. 'If the street ain't clear in ten seconds I'll throw you all in jail for disturbing the peace. Get out of here, and make it quick.'

'They said they were gonna lynch Joe Allen,' someone shouted, and there was an angry murmur of agreement.

'Nobody is gonna do anything. Clear the street now Leake — ' Kennett saw the liveryman's face in the crowd. ' — get Doc Mitchell over here.'

The crowd dispersed, leaving Mrs Morrison standing forlornly in the background and the two Circle B punchers on the ground. Goymer was sitting up, holding his head in his hands. Downey was unconscious; blood was seeping into the dust from his shoulder wound. Kennett glanced around. He saw Jake Blundell and Sarah emerging from the hotel, and grimaced when they moved along the sidewalk towards him.

'On your feet, Goymer,' Kennett rapped. 'We're gonna put Downey in a cell, and you can join him.'

'You can't jail us,' Goymer protested. He pushed himself to his feet, but wobbled slightly before finding his balance. 'Why the hell did you shoot

Downey? There'll be hell to pay for this!'

'You're right; there'll be hell OK,' Kennett agreed, 'and I'm the one who's gonna raise it. Get Downey up off the street and carry him into the jail.'

Goymer set himself, opening his mouth to protest, but Kennett cocked his pistol and scowled.

'You better change your mind before you say anything,' he cautioned. 'You're in enough trouble now without adding to it.'

Goymer dragged Downey upright and half-carried him into the office. Kennett motioned for Mrs Morrison to enter the office, pointed to the chair behind the desk, and she sat down thankfully. Kennett searched Downey, removed personal belongings from his pockets, and made Goymer empty his pockets before locking both men in a cell. When he went back to Mrs Morrison, Jake Blundell and Sarah were entering the office. Kennett fought down his dislike of the Circle B rancher. He detested the big man's arrogance and general bad temper.

Blundell was a powerful man in his early fifties, tall, tough, and self-opinionated. He was well known for shouting off his mouth. His fleshy face was set in angry lines, and his brown eyes were like those of a maddened bull as he glared at Kennett.

'Lew, what the hell are you up to?' he demanded. 'Sarah told me you let those outlaws take her out of here when they busted one of those killers loose. Is that the way you intend taking care of her when you two get married?'

'I wanta know what you're up to,' Kennett responded. 'How come you told Downey to put Joe Allen behind bars?'

'They caught him acting suspiciously on our range, and he pulled a gun and shot Murphy when they tried to grab him.'

'That's not what Joe told me.' Kennett shook his head. He looked into Sarah's pale face and saw that she was not pleased with him. 'Joe told me he was on his way to see you, Sarah. His mother sent him out to the ranch to pick up some material you wanted making into a dress. Is that true?'

'Yes.' Sarah nodded. 'Mrs Allen said she would send him out to collect the material.' She glanced at Blundell. 'What happened on the range, Uncle?' she demanded. 'Was Downey telling the truth about the incident or were the crew just having fun at Joe's expense, which got out of hand?'

'That's how Joe told it,' Kennett said, 'and I'm inclined to believe him. I'll hold him here until I can check out what he said. Jake, did you tell Downey to lynch Joe on Main Street if Murphy died?'

'The hell I did! Is that what Downey told you?'

'Did you hear shooting a few minutes ago?' Kennett countered.

'Yeah, and I figured it was you handling the crowd out here.' Blundell grimaced. 'I reckon that's where you've got to look to find who was talking up a lynching. Where are Downey and Goymer? I told them to keep an eye on things until you showed up. I didn't expect them to heap trouble on trouble. But if Joe Allen shot Murphy deliberately then he deserves all he gets.'

'I've jailed Downey and Goymer.' Kennett explained the situation, and saw Blundell's face take on a more belligerent expression. 'I'm gonna charge both of them with disturbing the peace,' he said firmly. 'Downey pulled a gun on me and I had to shoot him in the shoulder to disarm him. Why in hell would he wanta shoot me? That's what he was fixing to do. And Goymer assaulted a townsman. I'll decide on what to charge him with when I've talked to his victim. Sarah, do me a favour. Go along to the diner and tell Mrs Allen I want to talk to her.'

Sarah departed immediately, as if relieved to get out of Kennett's presence. Blundell paced the office a couple of times before rounding on Kennett.

'This won't do,' he snapped. 'I'm gonna ride into Fairfax and have a word with the sheriff. He won't be pleased to know you let a gang of outlaws come in here, turn a killer loose, and then ride off with my niece as a hostage.'

'When you see the sheriff tell him I'd like an extra deputy in here for a couple of weeks,' Kennett said. He broke off when the street door opened.

Doc Mitchell appeared, and demanded, 'Who's been shot?'

'It's Mort Downey. He's in a cell.' Kennett paused and looked at Blundell. 'I'll come back to you later, Jake. I'm not happy how this affair was handled by Circle B. If I find that your crew was having fun at Joe Allen's expense then I'll make an example of them. And they'll be in serious trouble if Murphy dies, not Allen.'

Blundell snorted and turned to depart without further comment. Kennett led the doctor into the cell block and unlocked the door of the cell containing the two Circle B men. The doctor entered to attend Downey. Kennett turned to Joe Allen, who was standing at the door of his cell, gripping the bars. His face was ashen. He looked scared, shocked, and was shaking badly.

'Settle down, Joe,' Kennett advised. 'You don't have anything to worry about. Your mother will be here in a few moments and I'll bring her in to see you. Just sit quietly on your bunk. You'll be OK.'

Allen shook his head. His knuckles were showing white under the strain of gripping the bars. He was badly scared, and Kennett felt certain that he had not heard what was said to him. He went closer, pushed a hand through the bars to touch Allen's shoulder, and the youngster jumped like a scalded cat. He looked up at Kennett, his eyes large and unfocused.

'Sit down on the bunk, Joe,' Kennett repeated. 'Your ma will be here shortly. Take it easy. Were you carrying a gun today?'

'Honest to God I wasn't, Lew,' Allen

replied in a wavering tone. 'I don't own a gun. Why would I wanta carry one? I'd never shoot anyone even to save my own life.' He turned away from the door and dropped wearily on to the bunk.

Doc Mitchell finished his examination of Mort Downey's wound and emerged from the cell, shaking his head.

'I'll have to get him over to my office to take the bullet out, Lew,' he said as Kennett locked the cell. 'I'll send a couple of men over with a stretcher when I'm ready for him.'

'He'll be here waiting, Doc.' Kennett heard a wagon out in the street and followed the doctor to the door. Mitchell departed and crossed the street to his office. Kennett waited for Rex Morrison to get down from the wagon. 'Your wife is waiting in here for you, Rex,' he called, and the rancher came hurrying across the sidewalk.

Kennett looked in the back of the wagon at the body of Thad Cooper, and then turned to follow Morrison into the office. A woman called to him and he turned to see Dora Allen coming along the sidewalk. She was under forty, and had been widowed at an early age. She owned the diner next to the general store, and worked hard to provide for herself and her son. She was slim and dark, good-looking — a fine, hard-working woman.

'Hi, Mrs Allen,' greeted Kennett, trying to inject cheerfulness into his tone. 'Come on in. I've got Joe safe inside, and he ain't hurt in any way.'

'What happened out at Circle B?' Mrs Allen demanded, entering the office. Her face was harshly set and her dark eyes held a world of misery. 'Sarah said Joe had trouble with some of their crew out at the ranch. I knew I shouldn't have sent him alone. Men are always picking on him because he acts a bit young for his age. He's still a boy, Lew.'

'I know what the Circle B outfit are like, Mrs Allen. But they went too far this time. Don't worry, I'll sort it out. Go on through that door in the back wall. You can talk to Joe. He's upset by what happened. I'll be with you shortly. I've got something to handle out here before I can get around to Joe.'

Mrs Allen went through to the cell block. Kennett waited while Rex Morrison made a big fuss of his wife. The rancher eventually turned to Kennett, smiling broadly.

'Thanks, Lew, for getting Aggie back in one piece,' he said. 'What do you want me to do about Thad?'

'It'll help me if you'll take his body round to Ossie Noble's place. Tell Ossie I'll see him later. I've got to get out after the posse, but I'd better see what's to be done with Joe Allen before I ride. Tell me, Rex, have you seen any sign of rustlers on your range?'

Morrison shook his head. 'I ain't been bothered, but I heard tell that Henry Tate lost a few steers a couple of weeks ago.'

'Tate didn't come in to report it.' Kennett frowned.

'He reckoned he'd handle it person-ally.' Morrison laughed drily. 'And that's what I'd do if I caught rustlers on my grass. They'd stretch hemp on the nearest tree. That's the only way to handle rustlers.'

'That's not what the law says.' Kennett grimaced. 'You'd be in a lot of trouble if you stretched someone's neck, even if you caught him red-handed steal-ing stock.'

'I'd take my chances with the law.' Morrison turned to his wife. 'Come on, Aggie, let's get moving. I wanta get our business done and head on back to the ranch. There's no telling where those outlaws will turn up next. It's getting so no one is safe anywhere. The law ain't able to do much about them.'

'They won't be around much longer,' Kennett said firmly. 'I'm gonna pull out all the stops to get them.'

Morrison shook his head as he departed with his wife. Kennett sup-pressed a sigh and went through to the cells. He paused in the doorway and watched Dora Allen at the door of Joe's cell. Her hands were through the bars and she was stroking Joe's face as she tried to soothe him. He went to the door of the cell in which Downey and Goymer were incarcerated. Downey was still unconscious. Goymer was sitting on the foot of a bunk, staring at the floor between his feet.

'Tell me what happened on Circle B range, Goymer,' Kennett said.

The cowboy looked up at him for a few moments, and then shrugged. 'You heard what was said earlier. I got nothing to add to that.'

'Who fired the shot that hit Murphy?'

'Ask Murphy. He was on the muzzle end of the gun that fired it.'

'I'm asking you, and I want the truth.'

'I didn't see the shooting. I was looking the other way at the time.'

'Who else was present? You and Downey came into town with Joe Allen, but there were others present when Allen was confronted.'

'I don't recall. Ask Allen. I reckon you're gonna believe him, whatever we say.'

Kennett went to stand beside Mrs Allen. She glanced at him, badly worried.

'I'd like Doc Mitchell to take a look at Joe,' she said. 'He's badly shocked. He's a good boy, and lately he's been working much too hard.'

'Why don't you fetch Doc Mitchell over?' Kennett suggested. 'In the meantime I need to have a few words alone with Joe.'

She nodded and turned away. Allen seized her hand but she pulled free.

'I'll come back shortly, Joey,' she promised.

When she left the cell block, Kennett gazed into Joe's eyes and held his attention.

'Tell me again what happened when you met those men on Circle B grass, Joe,' he urged.

Joe considered for a moment and then shook his head. 'I can't remember now,' he said slowly. 'Those two in that cell were there, but I don't remember any of the others.'

'You'll have to do better than that, Joe, if I'm to get you out of this. Think back to when you were stopped. A man named Murphy dragged you out of your saddle, huh?'

'That's right.' Joe nodded, his expression clearing. 'He said I was a rustler and he was gonna kill me for stealing cows. He pulled a gun, and I grabbed it because I was afraid he would shoot me. The gun went off and he fell down. The other men caught me. They said the gun was mine and I'd fired the shot deliberately at Murphy. They said if he died I'd hang for it. But I didn't have a gun.'

Joe turned away from the door and dropped face-down on the bunk. Kennett gazed at him for several moments before shaking his head and returning to the front office. He sat down behind the desk and closed his eyes. His head was whirling and his brain seemed to be on fire. He sighed heavily. This job was getting on top of him. There was trouble coming at him from all directions, and he didn't seem able to handle it.

He looked up when he heard the street door open, and got to his feet when Mrs Allen entered the office, followed by Doc Mitchell. He escorted them into the cells and unlocked the door of Joe's cell. Doc Mitchell entered and began examining the youngster. Mrs Allen stood beside Kennett, and he reached out and touched her thin shoulder.

'Don't worry,' he said. 'I believe Joe's story of what happened. I'll get to the bottom of it, you can bet. I'm gonna have to keep Joe in here for the time being, until I can get the facts of what really happened. Anyway, he'll be safer in here, and you'll be able to come and see him any time you want.'

'Thank you,' she said.

'Lew,' a voice called, and Kennett turned quickly to see Frank Fallon, the mayor, standing in the doorway leading to the front office. 'I'd like a word with you if you're not too busy.'

Kennett nodded and they went into the office. Fallon's smooth face was haggard with shock. He dropped into a chair as if his legs had suddenly lost their strength.

'I just heard about Thad Cooper being killed,' Fallon said. 'What was he doing outside of town limits? Did you send him out to look for that gang of outlaws?'

'The hell I did!' Kennett spoke harshly. 'I left town last night on the trail of one of the Ivy gang, and when I got back this morning Cooper wasn't around. You know he was keen to be a deputy sheriff. He was always trying to change his job, overlapping his duties with mine.'

'So how did he get shot?' Fallon leaned his elbows on the desk and supported his head in his hands. He closed his eyes and remained motionless.

'He met up with the Ivy gang south of here.' Kennett explained the incident.

'So Cooper has a brother.' Fallon looked up quickly. 'Why haven't we seen him around before? Where is he now? Would he take on the job of town marshal? If he did it would rid me of a nasty headache.'

'You'll have to ask him about that.'

'Where is he?'

'He went off after the gang, and he'll likely get himself shot if he ain't careful. I told him to trail the gang and wait for the posse to catch up with him, but he had blood in his eye and I reckon he'll go for the gang soon as he sees them. He was wearing two guns, so I expect he's used to fighting.'

'I hope he will step into Thad's shoes. Bring him to see me when he gets into town, huh?'

'I'll be riding out shortly to join the hunt for the gang,' Kennett said. 'I'd better bring in a jailer until I get back. Thad used to do that chore when he was around.'

'You've got someone who will take over?'

'A couple of townsmen. Casper and Eke are always available to do the job when required. They'll work shifts between them.'

Doc Mitchell came out of the cell block and paused by the desk. He set down his medical bag on a corner and frowned as he looked into Kennett's face.

'Joe has had a bad shock and it's affecting him,' Mitchell said. 'What will happen to him? Did he shoot Murphy in cold blood?'

'That's what the Circle B crew are saying but I don't believe them. Joe's story sounds more like the truth. But I'm gonna hold him in jail for a few days. I don't like the way Downey and Goymer acted outside here a short time ago, and if Murphy dies then Joe's life might be in danger. And Downey pulled a gun on me! I don't know what's got into Jake Blundell lately. It ain't like him to let his outfit ride roughshod.'

'Murphy should pull through, barring complications,' Mitchell said.

'That's good news.' Kennett nodded. 'It'll take some of the heat out of the situation.'

Mitchell departed, but paused outside and stuck his head around the doorpost. 'I'll send for Downey in about thirty minutes,' he said. 'Will you be here then?'

'If I'm not then there'll be a jailer on duty,' Kennett told him. 'I'll warn him.'

Fallon got to his feet. 'Don't forget about Cooper's brother when he shows up,' he said. 'We sure need another town marshal.'

'I'm gonna ask the sheriff to send in an extra deputy for a few weeks,' said Kennett, heaving a sigh. 'I'm being run off my feet right now, and I've got a nasty feeling there's more bad trouble coming up. The Ivy gang ain't on this range for nothing. They're up to something big, you can bet.'

Fallon went off and Kennett returned to the cells. Mrs Allen was talking to Joe, and Kennett paused and waited for her to look his way. She smiled wanly when she caught his eye, and he felt a surge of sympathy for her.

'I have to leave the office for a spell,' he said, 'but you can stay as long as you like. I'll be riding out shortly, but I'll bring in a jailer to take care of things.'

'Thank you, Lew. I'd like to stay for a while longer.'

Kennett left the office and paused on the sidewalk to look around. He heaved a sigh and shook his head as he considered what had happened. He went along the street to where Frank Casper lived. Casper was past fifty years of age, and before he retired he had been a deputy sheriff in the town for a number of years. He liked to stand in as a jailer, and was steady and reliable. He was a tall man who carried his age well.

'I'll come along to the office in about twenty minutes,' Casper said eagerly when Kennett explained the reason for his visit. 'I'll need to tell Martha what I'm gonna do. She's out at the moment, making the rounds of the local ladies, but she'll be back shortly.'

Kennett went to the livery barn and found Leake forking straw into his loft.

'Get a spare horse ready for me, Noah,' Kennett said. 'I'll be riding out in about thirty minutes. I might be away several days. My horse is hitched in front of the law office. Fetch him in and take care of him.'

'I'll see to it,' Leake promised.

Kennett stopped off at the mercantile on his way back to the office. Ben Overman was serving a customer but caught Kennett's eye and nodded.

'Be with you in a minute,' he called.

'Put some provisions in a gunny sack — enough for several days, Ben,' Kennett said. 'I'll be back to pick them up when I'm ready to ride.'

Overman nodded. 'When are you gonna catch that thief who robbed me?' he demanded.

'I'll get round to it when I've got the time,' Kennett replied.

He left the store and stood out front for some minutes, looking around and wondering if there was anything else he had to do. He saw Frank Casper leave his house and head towards the jail. Then he saw Jake and Sarah Blundell emerge from the hotel. They paused on the sidewalk. Jake was talking fifteen to the dozen, and using his hands to emphasize his words. Sarah stood passively, listening without comment to what was obviously a browbeating. Then Jake went to his horse, which was standing at a nearby hitch rail, and swung into the saddle. Sarah remained motionless until her uncle was riding away at a walk along the street. A thrill ran through Kennett when she eventually turned in his direction, saw him, and waved a hand to attract his attention.

She came towards him resolutely, her face harshly set. He watched her intently, wondering why he loved her, and why she professed to love him, and he suspected that Jake had been talking to her about their relationship. He was aware that Jake had never really cottoned to him, but he and Sarah had been close friends for as long as he could remember, and he could not imagine life without her. He was aware also that his job took up too much of his time, that he should make an effort to see her more often, but his time was precious and the job of deputy sheriff had grown too large for one man to handle.

'Lew,' Sarah said as she came up. 'Are you riding to Fairfax today?'

He shook his head, and saw her lips compress. 'I can't make that trip today,' he replied. 'You can blame Jake for the change in my plans. The Circle B outfit have given me a lot of trouble. I had to plug Mort Downey to prevent him shooting me. I can't believe this is happening. Why has Jake taken such an extreme attitude? It looks like Joe Allen will be set up with a murder charge if Murphy dies.'

'Do you believe Joe's word against ours?' she demanded.

'I don't take sides.' He spoke with some bitterness. 'I'm guided by facts, and I have no idea yet what is going on. But I will get to the bottom of it — and talking of taking sides, I've had a nasty feeling for a long time that Jake is against you seeing me.'

'I don't know where you get that idea from.' She shook her head firmly. 'Jake has always spoken highly of you. But getting back to Joe Allen, he has been out on the range a number of times lately. He's been seen in several different places, and each time afterwards cattle have been stolen from where he was observed.'

Kennett shook his head. 'I can't believe that. Where did you get that information from?' He looked along the street in the direction Jake Blundell had taken. The rancher had reined in at the bank and was sitting his horse, looking down at John Busby, the banker, who was standing on the sidewalk. 'Is your uncle on his way back to Circle B?'

'He's going to call in on some neighbours first, but he'll be home around sundown. He's talking of getting to grips with the rustlers.'

Kennett glanced along the street in the opposite direction. The town was quiet. He spotted a sudden movement in an alley mouth some fifty yards down on the opposite side of the street and saw a man step out of the alley, holding a rifle in his hands and looking along the street. The rifle began to level. Kennett expected a shot to be fired at him and moved without thinking to thrust Sarah into the doorway of the store, using more strength than he intended.

He drew his gun smoothly as he dived flat on the sidewalk, and lifted it into the aim as the rifle cracked. He fired a snap shot in return, and gun smoke flared from the muzzle of his .45. The crash of the shot hammered along the street.

He realized, as he fired, that the rifle was not aiming at him. He pushed himself to one knee and glanced along the street to the right, and his teeth clicked together when he saw Jake

Blundell in the act of falling out of his saddle. He looked back to the alley mouth and saw the man with the rifle lying on the ground.

'Quick, Sarah, I think Jake has been shot,' he called as he went at a run along the street.

The ambusher was lurching to his feet. Kennett fired again as the man faded back into the alley, and his slug tore splinters from the building on the corner. Trouble was beginning to pile up, he thought remotely as he went in pursuit, and he needed to discover quickly what was going on.

4

The sharp smell of gun smoke filled Kennett's nostrils as he reached the alley. He flattened against the wall and risked a quick glance around the corner. A discarded Winchester was lying a few feet inside the alley, and a man was on the ground at the far end. Kennett ran along the alley, his gun covering the inert figure. He slowed a few yards away and approached cautiously. The man was unconscious. Blood was seeping from a wound in his upper body. Kennett bent over him and used his left hand to turn the figure on its back.

He was shocked to recognize the ashen face of Mack Forster, a townsman who worked as a carpenter at the local timber yard which was on the back lot behind the alley. Forster seemed to be seriously hurt, and

Kennett ran back to the street end of the alley and peered around the street. Several men were appearing on the sidewalks, attracted by the shooting, and Kennett called to the nearest.

'There's a man hurt in the alley,' he called. 'Fetch Doc Mitchell to him.'

He did not wait to see if his order was obeyed but set off at a run along the street to where Jake Blundell was lying in the dust with Sarah bending over him. A crowd was gathering on the sidewalk in front of the bank. Kennett was breathless by the time he reached the spot, and his eyes took on a bleak expression when he saw that Blundell was seriously hurt. There was blood on his shirt front. He was unconscious. His face was ashen in shock. Sarah had opened Jake's shirt and was attempting to stanch bleeding from the bullet wound in the chest. She looked up at Kennett's approach. Her face was filled with a blend of desperation and shock.

'Is the doctor coming?' she demanded.

'I've sent for him,' Kennett replied.

'He'll be along shortly. Try and stop the bleeding, but don't move him. I'd better get back to the man who shot Jake.'

'Did you get him?' Sarah demanded.

'He's down in an alley and badly hurt,' Kennett replied. 'He's a towns-man called Forster and I'll need to know why he shot Jake deliberately from ambush.'

He went back along the street at a walk, his lungs seared by his quick action. He saw Doc Mitchell coming along the street and beckoned him to hurry. They reached the alley mouth almost at the same time.

'Jake Blundell is down in front of the bank, Doc,' Kennett said. 'Go to him first. The man in here shot Blundell. I'll stay with him until you get back.'

Mitchell nodded and went on along the street. Kennett hastened back to where Forster was lying, and discovered he was dead. Kennett heaved a ragged sigh as he straightened and looked around. Several men were entering the alley at the street end. He left the alley and looked across the back lot in the direction of the timber yard. A couple of men were standing in the wide gateway there, attracted by the sound of shooting. One of them was Charlie Hungate, the timber yard owner. Kennett waved a comeon signal and Hungate hurried over to the alley mouth.

'I've got Forster in here, Charlie,' Kennett said. 'He just shot Jake Blundell.'

'Forster did?' Hungate, a tall, lean man around forty, with dark hair and piercing brown eyes, stepped to one side and looked past Kennett. He uttered an expletive when he saw the motionless body.

'Is he dead?' Hungate demanded in a shocked tone.

'Yeah, dead as a doornail! Have you got any idea why he would shoot Blundell?'

'Me?' Hungate shook his head. He put out a hand against the wall at his side and leaned his weight against it.

'Hell, no! He's been working here all morning, hard at it, never stopped. He didn't look like he was intending to shoot someone.'

'How did he come to be in the alley with a rifle?'

'Who saw him? All he said to me was he had to go to the store for a sack of nails. I didn't see him with a rifle. Heck, why would he bring a rifle to work?'

'I saw him!' Kennett exhaled sharply through his nose. 'When I spotted him in the alley mouth at the street end, he was levelling a rifle in my direction. I was in front of the general store and I thought he was after me. But he fired along the street and hit Jake Blundell, who was sitting his horse in front of the bank. It was a deliberate shot. Forster knew who he was shooting at.'

'Is Blundell dead?'

'No, but he's in a bad way. The doc is with him now. Tell me about Forster. I've seen him around town, but I don't know much about him.'

'He's worked for me more than five

years, and I've never had a better worker. He's married, and Mrs Forster is expecting their first child in a couple of months. The way he was set up, I'd take odds against him getting mixed up in a shooting. Are you sure he did it?'

'It's beyond doubt,' Kennett said. 'Where'd he live?'

'One of those cabins at the south end of the street. There's a double row of cabins, and his is the second one in the back row.'

'Thanks, Charlie.' Kennett turned away. 'I'll talk to Mrs Forster now.'

'Take it easy with her, Lew,' Hungate said. 'This is gonna be a helluva shock to her.'

Kennett nodded and went back along the alley to the street. A dozen men were blocking the alley mouth. He pushed through them, ignoring their excited questions, and looked towards the bank, where another crowd was watching Doc Mitchell attending to Jake Blundell. For a moment he stood undecided, wanting to check on Forster. Then he saw Sarah standing forlornly beside the doctor, looking down at her uncle, and he went back along the street towards her.

Sarah looked up at him when he reached her side. Her eyes were wide, unblinking and filled with shock. She clutched at his arm with both hands and leaned against him. He slid an arm around her shoulders and drew her close.

'Lew, I think Uncle Jake is gonna die!' she whispered. A sigh gusted through her. 'What's going on? All this trouble that's breaking out! Do you know what's happening?'

'I've seen signs of trouble coming,' he said, 'but I didn't expect shooting on the street and outlaws coming and going around town. I've got Mack Forster dead in an alley. He shot Jake. I've got to break the news of his death to his wife, but I'd better wait to find out how Jake is doing.' He released Sarah and bent beside the doctor. 'How is he, Doc?' he demanded.

'I'll take him to my office when I've

stopped the bleeding,' Mitchell said without looking up. 'I think he'll make it, barring complications. Did you get the man who shot him? Does he need my services?'

'No, he's a case for Ossie Noble,' Kennett replied. 'His name is Mack Forster. He worked for Charlie Hungate.'

'I know the man.' Mitchell got to his feet. His hands were stained with blood. 'Mrs Forster is pregnant. Be careful how you break the news to her.'

Kennett nodded. He studied Sarah's face, wondering if she could stand up to the shock of what had happened. She shook her head slowly as she gazed at him. He put a hand on her shoulder and squeezed gently.

'I hate to leave you but there are things I got to do,' he said. 'Go with Doc and I'll come to his office when I get through. Take it easy. Doc says Jake will pull through, and you can take his word for it.'

'Go and do what you must,' she replied. 'I'll be OK.'

He left her then, shaking his head and wondering when he would be able to pursue the outlaws. He cursed Thad Cooper for leaving town, for deserting his duty. But Cooper was dead. He went along the sidewalk to the south end of town, and found five men standing outside the Forster cabin. A woman was in the doorway, remonstrating with them.

Kennett pushed through the men until he reached the one nearest the door, who was immoveable and shrugged off Kennett's thrusting hand. He was tall and solid, and turned swiftly with an aggressive expression on his face, which faded when he saw the law star on Kennett's chest. Kennett passed him and then turned to face the men. In the background of the raised male voices he could hear a woman sobbing inside the cabin.

'What's going on?' he demanded.

'These men are causing distress to Mrs Forster.' The woman standing in the doorway was middle-aged, tall and of strong build. Her large face was set in harsh lines. She was waving her clenched hands as if daring the men to defy her.

Kennett looked at the five men. He didn't know their faces. They stared at him defiantly, not prepared to back down.

'Well?' Kennett demanded, staring into the big man's eyes. 'What's your business here? Who are you?'

'I'm Bull Hamner,' the big man said. 'We work for Circle B.' He was dressed in stained range clothes but didn't have the look of a cowpuncher. He had the earmarks of a man one should not tangle with. His expression was bullish, his thin-lipped mouth showing defiance. His brown eyes were cold. His right hand was down at his side, very close to the butt of the pistol holstered on his right hip. The other men appeared to be of similar stamp, and Kennett wondered why he had never seen them out at Circle B.

'What are you doing here?' he queried.

'Mack Forster lived here,' Hamner said in a gravel-like tone. His gaze was unblinking. He looked primed for trouble. Arrogance showed plainly in his face and edged his hoarse voice.

'So?' Kennett steeled himself. He eased backwards a step and dropped his right hand to the butt of his .45.

'We wanta know why the boss was shot. Forster had no reason to ambush Blundell, and we reckon to find out what's going on.'

'I'm checking on this business, and I don't need any help from you,' Kennett said sharply. 'Get out of here and stay away. What do you expect to learn from a woman whose husband has just been killed? And come to that, how did you find out so quickly that Forster shot Jake Blundell? He was killed only a few minutes ago, and I didn't see you around at the time.'

'News travels fast,' Hamner growled, his eyes glinting.

'Get out of here, all of you.' Kennett spoke with a rough edge to his tone.

'I've got a job to do and you're hindering me.'

Hamner gazed at him long and steadily. Kennett faced him down. When none of the men moved to obey him he half-drew his pistol.

'Perhaps I didn't make myself clear,' he grated, 'so pin your ears back. Get the hell outa here. If you ain't on your way in five seconds I'll jail the bunch of you for obstructing the law. Now move!'

Hamner nodded slowly, but dumb insolence was showing on his tanned face. He turned abruptly and walked away with deliberate strides. The other four men followed him. Kennett watched them until they disappeared along the street.

'I thought you were going to have trouble with them,' said the woman in a frightened tone. 'They look like a bunch of hard cases to me. What do you think they wanted with poor Mrs Forster?'

'Who are you?' Kennett countered. He was wondering what was going on. At this rate he wouldn't get the opportunity to ride out after the posse and the outlaws.

'I'm Brenda Lacey. I live next door. I heard Mavis sobbing and came in to see what was wrong. Then those men turned up.'

'Who told Mrs Forster her husband was dead?' Kennett asked.

'It was Tom Keeble from the timber yard. He brought the news. You'd better come in.'

Kennett followed her into the cabin. He looked around the single room, which was sparsely furnished with a bed in one corner, a rough pine table, two chairs, and three hanging cupboards on the timber walls. The floor was boarded in pine, and the place was scrupulously clean. Mrs Forster was seated at the table, her arms on the woodwork, cradling her head. She was sobbing unrestrainedly. Kennett could see she was heavily pregnant.

Mrs Lacey crossed to the table and placed a gentle hand on the sobbing woman's shoulder. 'Mavis, the deputy is here. He needs to talk to you, dear.'

It was some moments before the sobbing ceased. Then Mrs Forster raised her head. She took a handkerchief from a pocket in her dress and dabbed at her eyes. She looked at Kennett, her gaze unfocused, as if she did not really see him. Mrs Lacey patted her shoulder gently and spoke in a gentle tone.

'Be strong, Mavis,' she advised in a kindly tone. 'You've got to think of the baby.'

Animation flickered to life in Mrs Forster's tearful eyes. She straightened her shoulders. Her hands trembled as she made an effort to regain her poise.

'Tell me it's not true,' she pleaded. 'Please say it's all a mistake. Mack can't be dead.'

Kennett crossed to the table and sat down opposite her. He leaned forward and held her gaze. Her mouth was agape. Shock was plain in her blue eyes. She looked ravaged by the tragic news she had received, but Kennett could see that in normal times she was a very attractive woman. Her long hair was straw-coloured. Her features were quite pleasing to his gaze.

'I'm sorry, Mrs Forster,' he said in a low tone, 'but the news you received is true. Your husband is dead. He was shot when he ambushed Jake Blundell, the Circle B rancher, on Main Street a short time ago.'

'Is Blundell dead?' she queried.

'He's badly hurt, but the doctor thinks he will live. I have to ask you some questions. I need to know why Mack ambushed Jake Blundell. Has there been any trouble between your husband and Blundell?'

'I don't know,' she replied haltingly. 'Mack never mentioned Blundell's name. But if Blundell is a rancher then there might have been trouble between them over cattle.'

'What kind of trouble?' Kennett frowned.

'Mack always wanted to start up his own cattle ranch. He dealt in stock in a small way in his spare time — buying and selling a few head at a time and saving the money to put down on a little spread of his own.'

Kennett grimaced. 'Can you tell me anything more about Mack's cattle business?' he asked.

'Mack could have told you but he's dead.' She began to cry again, and Kennett shook his head and changed his mind about asking more questions.

'I think you'd better go,' said Mrs Lacey. 'Mavis is not really up to talking. She's so shocked she doesn't know what she's saying. Why don't you come back in a day or two? She'll be over the first shock then, and you might get some sense out of her.'

Kennett nodded and got to his feet. He paused, regarded the stricken woman, and then shook his head and departed. He stood outside the cabin in silent speculation for several moments before returning to the main street. He went along to the doctor's house and pushed through the small crowd of townsfolk waiting at the door for news of Jake Blundell. Questions were asked of him as he entered the house but he ignored them. He needed answers to some questions that were bothering him.

Sarah was seated on a chair outside the doctor's office, hunched over with her head in her hands. Kennett paused and studied her for a moment, shaking his head. Filled with a rush of sympathy, he went to her side.

'Sarah.' He spoke gently. She looked up quickly, uttered a low cry at the sight of him, and sprang to her feet to throw herself into his arms. He held her close while she cried, patting her shoulder, aware of the shock and misery she was suffering. 'What's the latest on Jake?' he asked.

She looked up at him. Her eyes were misty with tears. 'Doc says he should be OK,' she replied, 'but it will be a long job.'

'Sit down again and I'll have a word with Doc,' he said. 'I need to know what's going on.'

He eased her back on to the chair and opened the door to the office, entered and closed the door behind him. Doc Mitchell, wearing a long white coat, was bent over the inert figure of Jake Blundell, who was stripped to the waist and lying unconscious on an examination couch. Mrs Mitchell, a trained nurse, was assisting her husband in the operation to remove the bullet from Blundell's chest. Kennett paused by the door and waited for the doctor to speak.

Doc Mitchell cast a glance in Kennett's direction. 'I'll be with you in a couple of minutes, Lew,' he said, and returned his attention to the wounded man.

Kennett remained motionless and silent, suddenly aware that his head was throbbing. He tried to relax until the doctor straightened. Mitchell dropped a misshapen bullet into a metal dish and handed a bloodstained instrument to his wife. He looked at Kennett, smiling.

'That's the worst part over,' he commented. 'We'll bandage him and hope the good Lord will do his part in Jake's recovery. There's nothing more I can do for him.'

'Do you think he'll live?' Kennett asked.

'He's as strong as a bull. The bullet was lodged in a muscle, not a vital organ. I reckon he'll be up and about in a couple of weeks, all being well. Have you any idea why Mack Forster shot him?'

Kennett shook his head. 'I'm making inquiries, but on the face of it there's nothing to go on. Forster just walked out of the timber yard on the pretext of getting a sack of nails from the store. No one saw him with a weapon before the shooting, but suddenly he's in the alley with a rifle, and he shot Blundell deliberately. I actually spotted him emerging from the alley, saw him fire the shot, and I hit him with my first slug as he disappeared back into the alley.'

'You hit him with your first shot?' Mitchell demanded. 'How many shots did you fire at him?'

'Two. The first one hit him; the second tore some splinters out of the building on the alley corner. I didn't get a chance to fire again because he went back into the alley. I followed him up and found him lying on the ground at the back end of the alley. It looked like he was making his way back to the timber yard.'

'Are you sure about hitting him with one shot, Lew?'

'Sure I'm sure! Why?'

'I took a quick look at him on my way back here,' Mitchell said, 'and noticed that he had been shot twice. One bullet hit him in the right side of the body; chest high. The second bullet got him squarely in the chest from his front.'

Kennett frowned as he stared into the doctor's grey eyes. Mitchell nodded slowly, aware of Kennett's surprise.

'My shot hit him in the right side,'

Kennett mused. 'Forster ran back along the alley towards the far end, so the second shot that hit him must have been fired from the back lot as he ran away from me.'

'Did you see anyone at that far end? I'm asking these questions because they will crop up at the inquest, and we'll need to know the answers, Lew.'

'This gets more complicated by the minute.' Kennett shook his head. 'I saw Charlie Hungate on the back lot, looking out from the timber yard. He must have heard the shooting and was looking out to see what had happened. Maybe he can throw some light on this.'

'I'm wondering why Forster shot Jake.'

'So am I, and that's what I'm gonna try to find out,' Kennett said. 'Sarah is outside the door, Doc. Have a word with her — reassure her about Jake, huh?'

'Sure, just as soon as I've bandaged him,' Mitchell replied.

Sarah got to her feet when Kennett

emerged from the office, her eyes showing hope. He grasped her shoulders.

'Jake is doing all right, Sarah. You'll be able to see him shortly. The bullet didn't hit him in a vital part, and he should be up and about in a couple of weeks.'

'That is good news!' Sarah lowered her head for a moment, and tears flooded her eyes. But she smiled, and Kennett patted her shoulder.

'I'm sorry I can't stay with you. I've got a lot to do. You'll be staying in town, I reckon, so I'll look you up when I get the time. Try not to worry too much. Jake will take this in his stride, you'll see.'

She nodded, and Kennett turned away. Then he paused and looked at her, and his tone was casual when he spoke.

'There's just one thing you might be able to help me with,' he said. 'I met five cowpunchers down at the Forster cabin. One of them is called Bull Hamner. He said they were riding for

Circle B, but I've never seen them around before, and they didn't look the kind of men Jake would employ. Do you know anything about them?'

'I'm afraid I can't help you, Lew.' She shook her head. 'Jake doesn't talk to me about ranch matters. You've got Downey and Goymer in jail, so why don't you ask them? Downey is the ranch foreman, so he should know something.'

'Thanks. I'll have a word with him shortly. See you around, Sarah.'

He departed and walked back to the alley where Forster had ambushed Jake Blundell, his curiosity aroused by Doc Mitchell's finding that Forster had been shot twice. Kennett paused in the alley mouth and recalled the tense moments of the shooting. He had fired twice at Forster, his first shot hitting the man in the right side. His second shot had clipped the corner of the building as Forster fled into the alley. He looked for the bullet hole and found it shoulder high in the sun-warped boards.

He walked into the alley, looking

around critically although there was nothing untoward to see. Forster had fled along the alley until he collapsed just before reaching the back lot. So how had he collected a second bullet? Kennett looked at the big building on the right-hand side of the alley. It was Mike Attew's slaughterhouse. There was a corral on the back lot and a butcher shop out front on the street. Kennett moved on to about halfway along the alley, and paused at a door that gave access to the rear of the butcher shop. He tried the door and found it was locked.

He recalled that Mack Forster had dabbled in a small way in buying and selling cattle, and his alert mind immediately fastened on the fact that here was a business that dealt in beef right on the scene of the shooting. Was there a connection? A strand of excitement began to unwind in the back of his mind. Was this where Forster had picked up the rifle he used to shoot Jake Blundell? He hadn't carried one when he left the timber yard to go to the store to fetch a sack of nails.

He tried the door again but it did not budge, so he walked back along the alley to the street and went to the door of the butcher shop. It was closed, and he hammered on the door with his knuckles. When there was no reply he kicked the bottom of the door with the toe of his right boot. He could see the interior of the shop, and was aware that it was closed every afternoon. There was no meat hanging up inside and the place had been washed and cleaned. He went back into the alley and walked through to the back lot. There was a small holding pen that led into the slaughterhouse, and he entered to look for Mike Attew, the butcher.

An inner door opened into an area where cattle were slaughtered. A metal rail contained hooks that were fixed to it by small wheels. The bodies of three steers that had been slaughtered recently were suspended from the hooks, and Mike Attew, a tall, powerfully built man in his fifties, blue-eyed and with fair hair, was busy skinning one of the animals. He looked up quickly when Kennett called to him, and straightened and stretched his back. He was holding a long skinning knife in his right hand. A long rubber apron protected his body, and his feet and lower legs were protected by rubber boots. His hands and forearms were covered in blood.

'You startled me, coming in like that,' Attew said. 'What do you want?'

'Didn't you hear the shooting outside a short time ago?' Kennett demanded.

Attew shook his head. 'These walls are thick.' He shrugged. 'What was the shooting about?'

'Mack Forster shot Jake Blundell.' Kennett watched Attew's face intently, but saw no reaction to his words.

'Someone is always getting shot around here these days,' Attew remarked. 'It's got so gunplay is becoming a part of everyday life. Is there anything you want or are you just asking questions? I've got to get on. There's a lot to do before

I can call it a day.'

'You've got a side door leading into the alley,' Kennett said. 'Is it always locked?'

'It's not a part of this business. It's the side door to the butcher shop.'

'Who works the shop when it's open?'

'My wife.' Attew took a fresh grip on his skinning knife and turned back to the steer he was working on. 'The shop is closed now, but Lizzie will be in the apartment over the shop. There's a private door beside the shop door on the street.'

'Before you get started again, answer me one question,' Kennett said. 'Where do you get your beef from?'

'Wherever I can buy it cheap. There's not much profit in this business. I have to cut costs where I can.'

Kennett moved closer to the half-skinned steer and looked for the brand. Attew came towards him, his face changing expression.

'What are you looking for?' he demanded.

'I'm checking on reports of cattle-rustling on the local range,' Kennett said. 'What puzzles me about it is that only a small number of steers are being stolen at any one time.' He looked into Attew's grim face. 'Normally rustlers run off a whole herd, but someone is working the range in a small way, and it came to me that a man like you would buy half a dozen steers at a time.'

'Are you accusing me of being involved in rustling?' demanded Attew truculently. 'I've been in this business nigh on thirty years.'

'I'm not accusing you of anything.' Kennett shook his head. 'Like I said, I'm checking on rustling, and I have to look in unlikely corners. Has anyone approached you recently with an offer of cheap beef on the hoof?'

'No, they ain't, and I wouldn't touch stolen stuff, so don't come prying round here trying to catch me out.'

'Keep your hair on! Just answer my question.'

'What question is that?'

'Where do you get your beef from? Give me names. Have you ever bought any from Mack Forster?'

'Who's Mack Forster?'

'You don't know him?' Kennett raised an eyebrow. 'He worked in the timber yard out back, and dabbled in buying and selling steers, so I heard.'

'I've had no dealings with anyone like that. My son Brad does the buying for me. Go talk to him about that side of the business. I just kill the steers and cut them up.'

'I'll talk to him, but just one more question before I leave. Why has the brand of that steer you're working on been cut out, and where is it? What have you got to hide, Attew?'

Attew cursed and lunged forward at Kennett, his right hand, gripping the skinning knife, sweeping in fast in a looping blow that was intended to stab Kennett in the stomach. Kennett sidestepped quickly, his left hand lifting to parry the blow, but as he did so his foot slipped on the bloodied floor and he lost his balance. As he fell, the sharp edge of the knife slashed along the length of his left forearm and blood spurted instantly.

5

Kennett had been on guard for tricks, and was not completely surprised by Attew's reaction. He landed on his back on the floor and kicked at Attew with both feet as the big man renewed his attack. His boot heels slammed into the butcher's ample stomach. Attew went over backwards, yelling in pain, and dropped the skinning knife as he fell. Kennett could feel acute pain in his arm, and blood was spurting. He rolled on to his left side; his right hand clawed for the butt of his holstered pistol. He drew and levelled the weapon, as Attew started to his feet, and covered the big man's chest with the muzzle.

'Hold it right there,' rasped Kennett, pushing himself to his feet. His gun did not waver in its aim.

Attew halted under the menace of the pistol, but he was barely restrained.

111

Kennett moved in close, and lashed out with his gun, slamming the long barrel against Attew's skull. Attew groaned and dropped to his knees. Kennett, mindful of the blood pouring from his slashed arm, struck again, and Attew went down headlong and lay senseless.

Kennett holstered his gun and checked his left arm. The knife had slashed him from elbow to wrist and the wound was gaping. He gripped the gash with his right hand to close it and ran from the slaughterhouse, hurrying along the back lots to the rear of the doctor's house. The back door was locked and he ran around to the front door, calling for the doctor as he hurried inside.

Sarah was still seated outside the doctor's office, and she jumped to her feet when Kennett entered the house. She gasped at the sight of blood on his arm.

'What's happened?' she demanded.

'Doc,' Kennett shouted. 'Where are you?'

Doc Mitchell appeared in the doorway of his office. He took in the scene and reached out to grasp Kennett's right arm.

'In here,' he said, guiding Kennett into the office. 'Sit down at the table.'

Mrs Mitchell was attending to Jake Blundell, still unconscious on the table. She looked up, took in the situation at a glance, and came to Kennett's side. She gripped the area of the knife slash with both hands and exerted pressure along the length of the wound, stanching the flow of blood.

'Hold it like that,' Doc Mitchell said, 'while I stitch it. This will hurt like hell, Lew,' he warned.

'Get on with it,' Kennett said sharply. 'I need to get back to the man who did it before he comes to his senses.' He was aware of Sarah standing in the doorway of the office, watching him intently, her face pale with shock. 'You'd better sit down, Sarah,' he warned. 'You don't look too good. I'm OK. It's just a little cut.'

Doc Mitchell chuckled and set to work with a needle. Kennett clamped his teeth together and bore the ministrations stoically. The wound was closed and Mrs Mitchell swabbed the blood from Kennett's arm. The doctor bandaged the wound. Kennett started to his feet immediately.

'Thanks. Doc, I'll see you later. I've got to make an arrest.'

'Is it anyone I know?' Mitchell asked.

'I got too close to the slaughter-man's knife,' Kennett replied, and hurried out of the office. He paused beside Sarah, who had returned to the chair outside the door, and patted her shoulder. 'I'll be in the law office in a few minutes,' he said. 'Why don't you go over there and make us a cup of coffee? The jailer will let you in.'

She nodded, instantly relieved, and departed.

Kennett let himself out of the house by the back door and went back to the slaughterhouse. He found Attew still slumped on the floor where he had left him. He paused, breathing heavily. The pain in his arm was becoming intolerable. The limb was throbbing vibrantly, and small patches of bright-red blood were beginning to show through the heavy bandage. He undid a couple of buttons on his shirt and inserted his left hand into the opening, finding some relief from the new position of the arm. He dropped his right hand to the butt of his gun and kept an eye on Attew while he glanced around the slaughter-house.

A half-filled gunny sack under a bench attracted his attention. He dragged it out, upended it and pieces of hide fell to the floor. They bore different cattle brands, and had obviously been cut from slaughtered steers.

Attew groaned and Kennett went over to the man, covering him with his gun.

'On your feet, Attew,' he said. 'You're on your way to jail.'

Attew staggered to his feet. He reeled and almost fell, and Kennett moved back out of distance, ready for trickery. Attew said nothing. He regained his balance and walked out of the building into the alley. Kennett followed him to the law office.

Frank Casper, acting in his capacity as jailer, locked Attew in a cell. He came back to the office with a grin on his face.

'What are the charges against Attew?' he asked.

'Assault, suspicion of rustling, and anything else I can think of.' Kennett looked up as Sarah emerged from the small kitchen at the rear of the office. She was carrying a tray which contained a coffee pot and three tin cups. She smiled wanly at Kennett, her face showing vestiges of shock and fear. 'Cheer up,' he said. 'It may never happen.'

She set the tray on the desk and busied herself pouring coffee. 'Who have you arrested on suspicion of rustling?' she asked. 'I heard what you said as I came in.'

'Mike Attew — the town butcher.' Kennett tried to ease his left arm into a more comfortable position and a grimace of pain crossed his face. He lifted a cup of coffee and gulped at the scalding liquid. 'Now I've got to pick up Attew's son Brad. It seems he's the one buying steers for slaughter, so I need to question him. He's the best lead I've got in this rustling business, and if Joe Allen has been hanging around with him then there might be something in what Downey said earlier about Joe acting suspiciously on the range. But I'm keeping an open mind. And I need to get moving. I should be out on the range chasing the Ivy gang instead of fooling around with petty crime.

'I didn't think Downey would lie about Joe Allen, although you wouldn't hear anything bad about him, Lew,' Sarah said. 'I've told you that I heard Allen had been seen around the range in suspicious circumstances. You've got to investigate in case there is any truth in what Downey said about Allen being mixed up in the rustling.'

'I'll get to the bottom of it,' Kennett promised. 'It looks like I've made the breakthrough I need.'

He went through to the cells and confronted Goymer. 'Have you got anything else to say about what happened on the range when you met up with Joe Allen?' he demanded.

'I've got nothing to say about anyone or anything,' Goymer replied. 'It's a waste of breath trying to tell you anything. Talk to Downey when he's awake. He'll give you the rights of it.'

Kennett moved along to the door of the cell where Attew was sitting on a bunk, his head in his hands. The butcher did not move. His eyes were closed and he was breathing heavily. Kennett imagined that the butcher was suffering a bad headache.

'What have you got to say about what happened in your place earlier?' Kennett demanded. Attew did not stir, but Kennett saw his eyelids flicker. 'I'm going out after your son now,' Kennett continued, 'and I'm hoping he's got more sense than you, Attew.'

He went back to the office and dropped heavily into the chair behind the desk. He wondered what was happening to the posse, and was worried that Gemmell would find more trouble than he could handle. But he could not be in two places at once, and his duty was to remain in town and try to clear up the trivialities besetting him. Sarah sat on a chair beside the desk, and Kennett sensed her gaze on him. He looked up, saw her troubled expression, and smiled to dissipate the tension. Then his expression hardened.

'There's something bothering you, Sarah,' he said, 'and I've been aware of it for some time now. Is it anything I should know about?'

'It's nothing,' she replied, shaking her head curtly. 'I'm worried about you, and that's all. I think it's about time you gave up this job and came out to Circle B to work. Life would be much simpler if you'd agree to that.'

'I'd like nothing better,' he replied, 'but I can't walk out on this job while there are problems to be solved, and Jake certainly wouldn't like to have me around on the ranch, cramping his style.'

'This job is too much for one man, and you're too pigheaded to ask the sheriff for some help.' Sarah warmed to her favourite subject, and Kennett suppressed a sigh. 'You haven't even got a town marshal now to handle the trouble in town. You're stuck here running around in circles while your real job, out on the range, is getting more and more out of hand.'

'So that's what you think!' He nodded. 'And I thought I was beginning to make headway. Well, I ain't one to change horses in midstream so I'm stuck with what I've got, and I'll try and muddle through until I get it right and finish it.' He got to his feet and went to the door, opened it and paused to look back at her. 'I wish you'd go out to the ranch and stay there until this trouble is over,' he said.

'I won't leave while Uncle Jake is lying helpless on his back,' she replied.

Kennett shook his head and crossed the street to the butcher shop. He tried the door that gave access to stairs leading to the apartment above the shop, found it locked, and knocked loudly. He heard the sound of a window above being thrust open, and stepped back until he could see Mrs Attew looking down at him. She was a big woman, heavy-faced, with a mop of black hair. Her fleshy face was lined with wrinkles and her eyes were deeply set under prominent brows.

'Oh, it's you!' she exclaimed. 'What do you want, Lew?'

'I have to tell you that I've arrested your husband,' he replied. 'He's in jail. I want to talk to Brad. Is he home?'

'What's Mike done?' she demanded. 'Don't tell me he was fighting drunk again.'

'It's more serious than that.' Kennett shook his head. 'He'll be in jail while I make some inquiries. Where's Brad?'

'I ain't seen him for a couple of days. He doesn't live here now. He's moved into Emma's guest house. You know where that is, I guess.'

'Sure. You can visit Mike if you want. Just tell the jailer I said you could see him.'

Mrs Attew shook her head and closed the window. Kennett went along the street to the guest house that was run by Emma Howes, a widow. Emma, an attractive blonde-haired woman in her late twenties, was standing on the doorstep talking to Dora Allen, and both women fell silent at Kennett's approach and looked at him intently.

'Sorry to interrupt,' he said, 'but I'm looking for Brad Attew and I heard he's living here now, Mrs Howes.'

'He moved in last week, but I haven't seen him for several days, Lew,' she replied. 'I think he's on a business trip.'

Kennett nodded. He turned his attention to Dora Allen. 'Did you get Joe calmed down at last?' he asked.

'He's much better now. Those rough cowpunchers gave him a bad time. It's about time they were pulled up by the law.'

'Joe is a friend of Brad Attew,' Kennett said. 'I'll be talking to Joe again later.'

'Try not to upset him,' cautioned Mrs Allen.

Kennett went on to the saloon and entered the dim interior. He paused and waited for his eyes to become accustomed to the gloom, and when he looked around at the half-dozen men standing at the bar he saw Brad Attew among them. Attew was tall and lean, dressed in a town suit and shoes. He had on a white shirt and a black string tie. A white Stetson was pushed back off his forehead to reveal a shock of curly black hair. He was wearing a cartridge belt which had a holster on the right side containing a Colt .45. The holster was tied down to the thigh with a leather thong.

The barkeep, Tom Jackson, was short

and sandy-haired. He was in shirtsleeves and a black bow tie, and wore a white apron over his clothes. He came along the bar to where Kennett was standing and grinned a greeting.

'Howdy, Lew, what'll it be? Say, you look like you lost a fight with a grizzly bear! What happened to your arm?'

'It's just a scratch,' Kennett said. 'Give me a whiskey, Tom. It's turning out to be one helluva day.'

'What's going on with Circle B?' Jackson picked up a bottle and a small glass and put them in front of Kennett. 'I heard there was talk of lynching but I can't believe Joe Allen has got himself in trouble. He's a hard-working youngster, not like some I could mention,' he added, glancing along the bar in the direction of the assembled men.

'It takes all kinds to make a community,' Kennett observed. He poured three fingers of rye whiskey and gulped it, relishing the fire it put in his throat and stomach. He set down the empty glass, slapped a coin on the bar and nodded at

Jackson. 'Thanks.'

He went along the bar until he was standing behind Brad Attew, who was talking to Chuck Busby, the banker's son. Attew glanced over his shoulder, saw Kennett, and stiffened.

'Is there something you want, Lew?' he demanded. His dark eyes were filled with suspicion.

'Yeah, I need to talk to you,' Kennett said. 'Come outside for a moment.'

'What have you been up to, Brad?' Chuck Busby demanded. He was in his mid-twenties and well dressed in a town suit. He worked in his father's bank as a teller. Kennett disliked him, for he had shown interest in Sarah in the past, until Kennett put him right about the situation.

'Anything you got to say to me you can say right here,' Attew said. 'I've just got in from Fairfax, and I'm parched. What's on your mind?'

'Your father is in jail.' Kennett paused for effect.

'What's he done now?' Brad Attew

laughed. 'Fighting drunk again, I guess, huh?'

'It's much worse this time,' Kennett replied. 'He's been buying rustled steers, and when I confronted him he attacked me with a skinning knife.'

Attew glanced at Kennett's left arm. 'Did he do that?' he demanded.

'That's why he's behind bars. And I found evidence in the slaughterhouse that he's handled rustled stock — a gunny sack half-filled with pieces of hide containing cattle brands cut out of the hides of the steers he's slaughtered recently.' Kennett half-turned to the batwings. 'You'd better come with me to the jail and we'll try and get to the bottom of this. I'll take your gun before we leave.'

'Are you arresting me?' Attew's face took on a grim expression and he dropped his right hand to the butt of his gun, a move which Kennett mimicked with his own right hand.

'I'm not arresting you,' Kennett said. 'It's just a matter of procedure. Lift your hand away from your gun and I'll take it. You'll get it back when you leave my office.'

Attew remained motionless for a moment, thinking it over. Then he lifted his right hand and Kennett took his pistol. Attew moved to the batwings and Kennett followed him. They went silently along the sidewalk to the law office. When they entered, Sarah got up from the seat behind the desk and Frank Casper picked up the bunch of cell keys.

'Have we got another customer?' Casper demanded eagerly.

'He's in for questioning,' Kennett replied. 'Sit down, Brad, and we'll get started.' He glanced at Sarah while Attew was seating himself. 'Perhaps you'd like to take a walk along the street until I get through here,' he suggested, and she nodded and departed.

Brad Attew settled on the chair placed before the desk, leaned back, and folded his arms. A half-smile played around his lips, but to Kennett's discerning gaze he seemed tense, and his eyes were bleak, as if he were expecting bad news.

'So what's this all about?' Attew demanded. 'I don't know a thing about the old man's activities. I just got in from Fairfax, and the first thing I heard was that Joe Allen is in jail, accused of shooting a Circle B puncher and suspected of rustling. Now you hit me with news of my father's arrest, and he's accused of buying rustled stock. What's going on around here, huh? What are you gonna tell me next, I wonder?'

'There's little doubt about your father's guilt,' Kennett said slowly. 'The evidence is there in the slaughterhouse, and when I questioned him about it he said you buy the steers he slaughters and sells in that shop of his.'

'He's not likely to admit buying stolen stock, is he? But I don't know why he's dragged me into it. Probably couldn't think of anything else to say on the spur of the moment, and if he was drunk at the time then he'd say anything to put you off.'

'He wasn't drunk,' Kennett said. 'So you're denying all knowledge of stolen stock?'

'I have no idea what is going on. Why don't you bring Pa out here and we'll soon get to the bottom of it.'

'I'm keeping you apart until I have statements from each of you,' Kennett said. 'So let's get down to cases. You're just back from Fairfax. What was your business there?'

'It was mainly a pleasure trip.' Attew grinned. 'That's all I'll say about it.'

'Mike said you buy the steers he slaughters for his business,' Kennett reiterated, 'and I see no reason to doubt his word.'

'You'll have to talk to him again about that. I haven't worked for him in a year. I got tired of the way he'd go off on a drunk every week. Anyway, I ain't cut out to be a butcher. I'm quite happy with my present job. It beats handling dead meat.'

'So what do you work at now?'

'I'm a salesman for Charlie Hungate, the timber merchant. I get orders for new buildings from all over the county. I got two orders in my pocket right now from Fairfax — one for six cabins to be built on the edge of town, and another for a new church hall for Preacher McPherson.'

'Charlie Hungate, huh?' Kennett nodded. 'Show me the orders.'

Attew nodded, reached into his inside pocket, and produced a slim notebook. He tossed it on the desk.

'There you are. It lists all the orders I've taken in the last six months.'

Kennett examined the entries and then handed the book back to Attew, who stood up immediately.

'Can I go now?' he demanded.

Kennett shook his head. 'No. I'm not satisfied yet. Mike made a serious allegation against you so just sit tight while I talk to him again.'

'It would be better if you let me talk to him,' Brad insisted. 'I reckon his brain is floating in rye whiskey, and he doesn't know what he's saying half the time. Why don't you talk to my mother? She washed her hands of him a long time ago. She'll tell you what he's really like.'

'Turn out your pockets and I'll put you in a cell until I've got some sense out of Mike,' Kennett said.

Attew protested vociferously but Kennett was adamant. He turned to the watchful Frank Casper.

'Lock him in that back cell beside the kitchen,' he instructed. 'Then fetch Mike Attew out here.'

Casper grinned and hastened to obey. Kennett sat thinking until Mike Attew shuffled out of the cell block and dropped into the seat in front of the desk. He leaned forward, put his elbows on his knees, and dropped his head into his hands. Kennett felt a stabbing pain in the knife slash in his arm and stifled any sympathy he felt for the hapless butcher.

'So what have you got to say for

131

yourself now you've had time to think about your situation?' Kennett asked.

Attew looked at him through his splayed fingers. He shook his head, and groaned at the effort.

'I don't know a damn thing about rustling cattle,' he growled. 'You need to talk to Brad. I told you he buys my stock. I never leave the butcher shop or the slaughterhouse, and that's a fact.'

Kennett grimaced. 'I've had a word with Brad already, and he denies all knowledge of buying cattle for you. So who brings the stolen steers into town? They come in off the range as and when you require them, huh?'

'You're talking to yourself.' Attew leaned back in the chair, folded his arms across his chest and closed his eyes. 'I need to sleep,' he complained. 'You gave me a helluva whack on the head.'

'It's no more than you deserved after slashing my arm,' Kennett retorted. 'Why in hell did you do that?'

'You annoyed me.'

'So let's get on. You're saying you didn't know the steers were stolen, is that it?'

'Now you're getting to it.'

'If that's the case then why did you cut all the brands from those hides?'

'I didn't want anyone getting an idea that the stock was stolen.' Attew grinned and then raised his hands to press his fingers against his temples.

Kennett sighed and motioned to the intent Casper. 'He's not talking sense, Frank. Lock him in the cell until he's had time to think things over. I'm going out to check on one or two details. I'll be back shortly.'

'What about Brad Attew?' Casper demanded.

'Leave him where he is until I get back.' Kennett got to his feet.

Casper took Mike Attew back into the cell block. Kennett waited until the jailer reappeared in the office before going to the street door. He was worried as he left the office and crossed the street to return to the slaughterhouse. He couldn't leave town right now, and yet he knew his first duty was to go for the Ivy gang.

He entered the alley beside the slaughterhouse and paused to look around, wondering what had happened to the rifle Mack Forster had used to shoot Jake Blundell. He went on to the far end of the alley and looked across at the timber yard. He could see Charlie Hungate talking to an employee in the yard, and crossed to the gate to attract Hungate's attention.

'You found some trouble with Mike Attew,' Hungate observed. 'I saw you run to the doctor's with blood spilling out of your arm. What was that all about, Lew?'

'Have you seen any of the cattle Attew slaughters being delivered here?' Kennett countered.

Hungate nodded. 'Sure. They come in at all times during the day or night.'

'Who delivers them? Is it anyone you know?'

'Nobody who lives around here, that's for sure. There are half a dozen men that drive the steers in, but no more than three come at any time. They look a rough bunch to me, and it's crossed my mind several times that they could be rustlers. They got that look about them. I wouldn't deal with them, but that's Attew's business.'

'But you never thought to tell me about them, huh?'

Hungate shrugged. 'They're a tough bunch.'

'Can you describe any of them? Have you seen them around town?'

'Yeah, there's one man who comes every time. I reckon he runs the business. He called here once to see Mack Forster, and they talked about cattle.'

'That figures. Why didn't you tell me about this, Charlie? You know I've been trying to get the deadwood on the rustlers.'

'It pays to mind your own business around here.' Hungate shook his head. 'And I don't get paid to do your job for you, Lew.'

'Thanks for nothing. Can you describe the man who spoke to Forster?'

'Big feller! I wouldn't want to tangle with him. He was range dressed, and wore two guns.'

Kennett got an image of Bull Hamner in his mind. He mentioned a few of Hamner's physical details and Hungate nodded.

'Yeah, that sounds like the feller I saw. Where did you see him?'

'He was making a nuisance of himself outside Forster's cabin when I went to tell Mrs Forster that her husband was dead. There were four other men with him. If I see them in town I'll want you to take a look at them. OK?'

'I don't wanta get involved, Lew. It ain't my job.'

'There's one other thing, Charlie. You've got Brad Attew working for you, huh?'

'Brad? Sure. He's bringing in a lot of business. He's got a nose for the job.'

'Does he work full-time?'

'Yeah, he covers a lot of ground, and

he's good at it.' Hungate paused and subjected Kennett to a close scrutiny. 'You got something on your mind, Lew?'

'I'm just asking questions, Charlie.'

'Brad is a good man! He's nothing like that drunken bum who spawned him. I'll stand up for Brad any time.'

'OK, I'll take your word for it.' Kennett took his leave and went back to the law office.

He picked up the cell keys and went into the cell block to confront Joe Allen, who was looking forlorn and worried. Allen got to his feet and came to the door of the cell.

'How long are you gonna keep me in here, Lew?' he demanded.

'I'm keeping you here mainly for your protection, Joe. There was talk of lynching you if Murphy died.'

'How is he?'

'Not good. You're in the best place right now. Tell me about your friends, Joe.'

'Friends?' Allen frowned. 'I don't

understand, Lew.'

'I need some background on you, so tell me what you do apart from working in the diner. Who do you see around town, and where do you hang out with them in your spare time. Have you got a girl, for instance?'

'I see Mary Turner sometimes, but I think she's sweet on Chuck Busby, the banker's son. Busby works in the bank and he gets more money than I do. He's got a fancy rig and two high-stepping sorrels. If Mary takes to him then I won't have a chance, unless I can make a pot of gold.'

'I've heard you're friends with Brad Attew. How'd you get along with Brad?'

'I was friends with him but since he's worked for Hungate he ain't around. And he's getting too big for his boots. I don't like him now.'

'Did you ever help him bring cattle into town for Mike Attew?'

'Yeah, before I worked full-time in the diner for my ma. It was pocket-money stuff. I've been trying to save enough dough to interest Mary Turner.'

'Where did the cattle come from? What I mean is, did they come off the local range and was they paid for?'

'Are you thinking it was stolen stock?' Allen frowned as he gazed into Kennett's impassive features. 'We never handled rustled steers, Lew. We worked as drovers. Mack Forster bought the cattle, and we drove them in for him.'

'But you haven't done it for some time now, huh? You've been working full-time in the diner. Who drives the stock in these days?'

'I've seen a rough bunch coming into town at times, and always with a few steers. They don't belong around here. I've seen one of them with Mack Forster, so why don't you talk to Mack about them? He's the man who does the deals with Mike Attew.'

Kennett nodded. 'Thanks for your help, Joe. Settle down now. I'll let you go soon as I think you'll be safe.'

Allen shook his head and returned to his bunk. Kennett looked into the cell where Downey and Goymer were housed. Downey was snoring loudly. Goymer sat motionless on his bunk, his back to the bars of the adjoining cell. He was staring into space.

'Hey, Goymer, tell me about the new men working for Circle B,' Kennett said.

Goymer jerked and straightened. 'What new men?' he demanded. 'There ain't anybody new that I know of. We've always been short-handed.'

'I met a man called Bull Hamner earlier. He told me he was working for Circle B — him and four other cowpunchers.'

'Oh, that bunch! They've got nothing to do with the regular crew.'

'Where do they hang out?'

'I don't know. But Bull Hamner sees a lot of Sadie Spandler, who works in Madison's Saloon. She's got a cabin on the back lot behind the saloon. If Hamner's in town then that's where he'll be.'

'Thanks.' Kennett turned away. 'I

need to talk to him.'

'Take my advice and don't tangle with him.' Goymer laughed. 'He's a long, curly wolf.'

Kennett departed and set out for the cabin behind the saloon. He needed more information on the cows that found their way into the slaughter-house, and there was only one way to get it.

6

As he made for the back lot behind the saloon, Kennett was keenly aware of his discomfort — the pain of the knife slash in his left arm and the niggling ache of a bullet crease in his left thigh. He did not feel much like confronting a hard case, but with the regular posse men out of town there was no one he could turn to for help. He drew his pistol, checked it, and returned it to his holster. He would do his duty.

He entered the alley beside the saloon and made his way to the back lot. There were a number of buildings dotted around, but only one cabin. He drew a deep breath as he made for it. A saddle horse was tethered to a post on the right-hand side of the building, and he didn't doubt that it belonged to Bull Hamner. He knocked on the cabin door and waited vainly for a reply. Moments passed before he knocked again with the same result. Impatience filled him but he subdued it, and was about to depart when he heard the wooden bar on the inside of the door scraping up. The door was opened a fraction and Sadie Spandler peered out at him, her blue eyes blinking rapidly in the bright sunlight.

'What do you want this time of the day, Lew?' She was tall with a good figure, but her looks were spoiled by the ravages of her way of life. She spent every night working in the saloon under glaring lamplight and breathing strong tobacco smoke. Her eyes were listless, her long blonde hair lank and lifeless-looking. She was wearing a long pink dressing gown, and looked as if she had been awakened from a deep sleep.

'Hi, Sadie,' Kennett replied, his tone friendly. 'I need to talk to a guy called Bull Hamner, and I heard he's seeing you these days. Is he around? I saw him in town earlier.'

'He was here but he ain't now,' Sadie

replied. 'Beat it. A gal needs her beauty sleep.'

'Is that his horse tethered to the side of the cabin?'

'I don't know. I guess he came on a horse. Don't tell me he's left it here!' Sadie opened the door, emerged from the cabin, and walked barefoot to the right-hand corner to look at the horse. 'Yeah, it's Bull's mount. Why has he left it here? He reckoned he was in a hurry to get out of town.'

'He might be in the saloon. I'll check.' Kennett turned away and walked back towards the alley.

He glanced over his shoulder as he entered the alley and saw Hamner emerging from the cabin. The hard case went to his horse, swung into the saddle, and came at a canter towards the alley. Kennett waited, his right hand down by his side, the inside of his wrist touching the butt of his holstered gun. Hamner came up and looked as if he intended riding Kennett down.

Kennett held up his hand. 'Hold up

there,' he said crisply. 'Did Sadie tell you I want to talk to you?'

'I don't want to talk to you,' Hamner growled. 'Get outa my way.'

'Climb down from that horse,' Kennett said sternly.

Hamner reined in, glared at Kennett, and a thin smile of derision appeared on his thick lips. He was holding his reins in his left hand and the fingers of his right hand hovered above the flared butt of his holstered pistol.

'You'll be dead meat if you make a play for your gun,' Kennett told him. 'Just do like I say, and get down from your horse.'

Hamner's grin widened, but his eyes remained cold, and Kennett sensed trouble looming. Hamner did not look like a man who would back down.

'Don't bring trouble on yourself just because I wanta talk to you,' Kennett advised.

'My business is no concern of yours,' Hamner snarled impatiently. 'And you look like you've had more than enough trouble for one day, so don't push your luck.'

'I'll tell you one more time — get outa that saddle and put your hands up. Ignore me one more time and I'll shoot you outa your saddle.'

For a fleeting moment there was silence and stillness between them. Kennett was hair-triggered, ready to pull his gun and enforce his order. Hamner was watching him intently, and Kennett could almost see the way the man's mind was working. Then Hamner decided that Kennett was not bluffing and uttered a short laugh. He stepped down from his saddle and raised his hands shoulder high.

'What's on your mind?' he demanded. 'Make it quick because I got things to do.'

'Turn your back and I'll pull your gun,' Kennett said. 'You can have it back when I've finished talking to you.'

Hamner shook his head and turned away. Kennett stepped in close and disarmed him.

'So what is this all about?' Hamner demanded.

'You've been delivering stock to Mike Attew the local butcher, and I've got a suspicion that the steers were stolen.'

'You're pushing your luck, Deputy, accusing me of rustling, but you've got the gun at the moment so I'll listen.'

'Tell me about your dealings with Mack Forster. You were outside his cabin earlier, when I went to tell Mrs Forster about her husband's death. Forster had shot Jake Blundell, and you are working for Circle B, so how do you fit in with Forster? I believe he's been stealing stock locally and selling it to the butcher.'

'Did you work that out by yourself?' Hamner demanded.

'I'll ask the questions,' Kennett answered. 'Just answer me, and your story had better be good.'

'Sure I work for Blundell, and he told me to bring that stock in to Attew. It was paid for, and Blundell has a bill of sale for every one of those steers.'

'And those steers that did not come from Circle B?' Kennett asked.

'I don't know a thing about them.' Hamner shook his head.

Kennett considered for a moment and then stuck Hamner's pistol back into its holster.

'Get outa here,' he said. 'I'll talk to Jake Blundell. You'd better watch your step, Hamner. I don't like the way you operate.'

Hamner smiled and swung into his saddle. He looked down at Kennett, and for a tense moment his right hand hovered above the butt of his gun. He was itching to pull the weapon, but the law star glinting on Kennett's shirt front deterred him and he touched spurs to the flanks of his mount and sent the animal into the alley. Kennett expelled his pent-up breath in a long sigh and eased his aching body. His muscles were stiff with anticipation, and he relaxed slowly from a high pinnacle of alertness. He was certain he had not seen the last of Hamner.

Returning to the street, Kennett stood looking around, wondering what to do next. He guessed he ought to try and talk to Jake Blundell, for he felt that the Circle B rancher knew the answers to some of the questions bothering him. He went to the doctor's house, and impatience filled him when he discovered that Jake Blundell was still unconscious and likely to remain so for another twenty-four hours.

When he returned to the street he heard the sound of rapid hoof beats. A rider was coming into town from the south. He recognized Rafe Milton, who had ridden out with the posse, and went towards the law office, reaching it as Milton came up. Milton was the town gunsmith, a short, serious-minded man whose only son had been killed in a gunfight a few years earlier. He always rode out with the posse when it was needed, and was a good man in a fight. He was dusty and breathless, and there was blood on his shirt front.

'What's happened, Rafe?' Kennett demanded. 'There's been trouble, huh? Where's the rest of the posse?'

'We had more damn trouble than we could handle.' Milton slid out of his saddle and wrapped his reins around a hitch rail. 'Those pesky outlaws ambushed us from Pendle's Ridge and shot the hell out of us. We were like sheep among wolves! Gemmell is down in the dust with two bullets in his chest. Henry Chilvers is dead, shot through the heart, and Sam Wenn is stretched out with a bullet in each leg. It was hell while it lasted, and we didn't stand a chance. They pinned us down and used us for target practice. I reckon they could have killed all of us if they were so minded. But they took off and left us. I've come in for a wagon to pick up the wounded. Asa McCall took Lenny Dawson and Al Smith out on the trail of the outlaws, but they weren't keen on doing it.'

'You look all in, Rafe. Get Leake to drive a wagon out there and then come and take over here in town from me, huh? I'll swear you in as a deputy. I need to ride out to see what's going on. Doc had better go with me.'

Milton nodded. He was tight-lipped. 'I'll see Leake and get the wagon started for Pendle's Ridge,' he said.

'Bring me a fresh horse from the barn,' Kennett told him. 'I'll alert Doc.'

He limped across the street and returned to the doctor's house. Mitchell looked up in surprise when Kennett entered his office.

'Are you OK, Lew?' Mitchell demanded.

'Far from it, Doc.' Kennett explained the situation out at Pendle's Ridge.

Mitchell sprang to his feet. 'I'll head out right away,' he declared. 'Are you riding out there?'

'Sure as hell I am! We'll ride together, Doc. Meet me at the law office when you're ready to ride.'

Kennett went back to the law office. By the time he had checked his weapons and explained the situation to Frank Casper, Doc Mitchell appeared. Then Rafe Milton returned.

'Leake is heading out right away, Lew,' Milton reported. 'I've got a fresh horse outside for you.'

'Will you act as a temporary deputy until I get back, Rafe?' Kennett asked.

'Sure thing. Swear me in.'

Kennett did so, and heaved a sigh of relief as he departed, followed by Doc Mitchell. They rode out of town, and Kennett, ignoring the pain of his wounds, set a fast pace along the trail, heading for Pendle's Ridge. His mind seemed to clear of the clutter of the recent activity in town — Mike Attew's arrest, the shooting of Jake Blundell, and Mack Forster's death. They paled into insignificance as he mulled over what had happened to his posse, and he reaffirmed his vow to wipe out the Hap Ivy gang.

*   *   *

Two hours elapsed before Pendle's Ridge, named after the rancher who had first raised cattle in the area, appeared on the skyline. Kennett suffered pain over the last stretch, as he and Doc Mitchell pushed their mounts up the long incline to the ridge, for his

152

arm reacted badly to the rigours of riding, and he had been compelled to slip his left foot out of its stirrup in an attempt to ease the pressure on his wounded left thigh. But he found no easement, and was intensely relieved when a rifle shot hammered from ahead and to their right and echoes fled across the seemingly illimitable Kansan prairie.

They slowed and went on towards a lone figure standing on a rock just below the crest of the ridge, and came upon the spot where the posse had been ambushed. Horses were tethered in undergrowth, and three motionless figures were stretched out on the ground — one of them hidden from view under a blanket. A figure came down from the ridge, carrying a rifle, and Kennett recognized Bill Jex, a posse man.

'What happened, Bill?' Kennett asked as Doc Mitchell hurried across to the two wounded men.

'There was hell to pay.' Jex was a small man, ginger-haired and slightly built.

'Milton told me.' Kennett's grim gaze went to where Doc Mitchell was bent over the big figure of Art Gemmell.

'I don't think Gemmell will make it,' Jex observed. 'He collected two bullets in the chest. I reckon he'll be dead before sundown. Chilvers was killed instantly. Wenn was hit in both legs. We managed to stop the bleeding, but he'll be crippled for life, if he makes it.'

'Milton said McCall, Dawson and Smith took up the trail of the outlaws. Are they still out looking?'

'I ain't seen hide nor hair of them since they left. I told them to stay here but they were all fired up by the ambush. I reckon they'll get themselves killed. We ain't any kind of a match for those bad men. When you go after them again, Lew, you'd better take twenty men along.'

Kennett nodded and crossed to Doc Mitchell's side. He looked down at Gemmell. The big blacksmith was unconscious, his massive chest soaked with blood. Mitchell looked up at

Kennett and shook his head. Kennett nodded and went to where Sam Wenn was lying. Wenn, a tall, thin man, was conscious and in considerable pain. He had a rough bandage around his left knee and another on his right thigh. He looked up at Kennett with bleary, pain-filled eyes. His teeth were clenched.

'How are you doing, Sam?' Kennett asked.

'OK, Lew,' Wenn said. 'You'll catch those murdering sidewinders, won't you?'

'You bet we will.' Kennett nodded. 'The doc's here. He'll make you comfortable, and a wagon is on its way. You'll soon be back in town.'

He went back to Bill Jex, who was sitting on a rock, gazing into space.

'Did you see which way McCall and the others rode when they went off, Bill?'

'They went over the ridge, but I couldn't tell you which way they went when I lost sight of them. There'll be tracks, I reckon.'

'There's a wagon coming out from

town so keep an eye open for it, and get everybody back to town. I'll see if I can find McCall and the others.'

Jex nodded and Kennett went back to Doc Mitchell, who was doing what he could for the blacksmith.

'I'm riding on, Doc,' Kennett said. 'Three of the posse went on after the outlaws and I've got to find them. I'll see you when I get back to town.'

'I should think you've done enough riding today,' Mitchell observed. 'But you know your business best, Lew. Just take it easy, huh?'

Kennett nodded and went back to his horse. He stifled a groan as he climbed into leather, and then went on up the ridge. The sun was now well over to the west, and shadows were beginning to show as he looked around for tracks. He found three sets of prints, well defined in thick dust, and followed them quickly. He settled down to the prospect of a long, hard ride, his keen eyes narrowed, his attention split between the tracks he was following and the trail ahead.

His thoughts meandered, and he tried to make sense of what had happened in town, but it was a puzzle that needed more information to be made available to him before he could begin to understand the situation. Sarah was immoveable in the background of his thoughts, and he could only wonder at what was bothering her. She certainly had something on her mind, and her general manner had changed in the past weeks, although he had not been aware of it until recently. But she was no longer the carefree girl he had fallen in love with. Something was affecting her, and he had been too wrapped up in his job to notice.

The tracks went on and on in the rough ground, and Kennett began to think that he would have to make camp when night came. Then he topped a rise and saw a horse some yards ahead, standing motionless with trailing reins. He jerked on his reins and reached for his gun, and then saw an inert figure on the ground near the horse. A cold chill stabbed through him. He approached carefully, dismounted with some difficulty, and peered down at the body of Al Smith, one of the posse men he was tracking.

Smith was dead with a bullet in his chest. He had been shot through the heart. A bitter sigh escaped Kennett. He shook his head and looked around. Shadows were thickening over the range but he could still read sign. There had been another ambush. He could see a patch of trampled ground where several horses had stood for a time, and then two animals had gone on in the general direction in which they had been heading.

Kennett checked the waiting horse, tied its reins together and looped them over the animal's neck, giving it freedom of movement. He returned to his mount and climbed into the saddle, determined to go on as long as he could see the tracks. The two surviving posse men had pushed on. He continued until he could no longer see the tracks clearly, and then halted to take stock of the situation.

He realized that he was within a couple of miles of a small horse ranch run by Abel Piercey, and his eyes glinted at the thought of hot food and fodder for his horse. He made a note of where he was leaving the trail and rode into the gathering darkness. Stars were twinkling overhead and a thin crescent of the moon in its first quarter shone in a cloudless sky. An hour later he spotted the yellow gleam of a lamp and made out the shape of a cabin.

He rode into a yard and hailed the cabin, remaining in his saddle. After a pause the door opened and a man appeared, silhouetted against yellow light.

'Who's there?' growled a husky voice.

'I'm Lew Kennett, Abel. I'm on the trail of outlaws.'

'Lew! Heck, you're just the man I wanta see.'

'What's happened?' Kennett demanded. 'Have you had trouble here?'

'I was gonna ride into town come sun-up to see you. Get down and come in, Lew. Hap Ivy and his bunch were here earlier.'

Kennett dismounted, and paused to wait until the worst of his pains subsided. Piercey remained in the doorway, bright yellow light silhouetting him. Kennett wrapped his reins around a post and went to the door. Piercey stepped back inside the cabin, allowing Kennett to enter. As he stepped across the threshold, Kennett became aware of a rapid movement to his left and ducked instinctively, his right hand dropping to the butt of his pistol. Then a solid object crashed against the left side of his head and lights exploded in his brain. He fell forward on his face, blackness swirling into his brain, and lost consciousness.

* * *

His first intimation of returning to his senses was the drone of voices cutting through the limbo into which he had descended. Pain was throbbing in his head. His wounds were hurting. He opened his eyes and then closed them quickly because the lamplight was too bright for his senses. He raised his right hand to shield his eyes and saw Piercey standing to one side, his bearded, face expressionless and yet giving the impression of fearful resignation. Mrs Piercey was standing in front of the stove with the outlaw Swig Rafferty at her side. Rafferty's right hand held a knife that was pressed against Mrs Piercey's throat.

Kennett blinked. The voices began to make sense as his head cleared.

'I reckon we better kill him right now,' someone was saying, and a pistol clicked three times as it was cocked. 'He shot me, and I owe him for that.'

'Lay off, Walton,' a harsh voice cut in, and Kennett frowned as he recognized it. Hap Ivy! 'I wanta know what he's doing out of town and riding in here on us. Just watch him. He's coming out of it. Keep your gun on him because he's a hard man. I wanta talk to him and hear what happened in town after we pulled out.'

Kennett tried to get up but his left arm refused to take his weight and he dropped back with a groan. He looked around and saw Ivy's intent face. The gang boss seemed irritated, and he motioned to Swig Rafferty to get Kennett to his feet. Rafferty grasped Kennett's left arm and pulled him up. Agonizing pain flooded the limb and Kennett yelled. He tried to pull away, and Rafferty punched him in the stomach and released his hold. Kennett fell back, gritting his teeth against the pain in his arm. Ivy stepped forward and thrust Rafferty away.

'I want him fit to talk.' Ivy reached down, grasped Kennett's right arm, and pulled him to his feet. 'Sit down on that chair at the table,' he continued, and steered Kennett to the right.

Kennett flopped into the chair and tried to relax. He grasped his left arm with his right hand and lifted the limb into a more comfortable position. He threw a quick glance at his holster and saw that his pistol had been removed. He stifled a sigh and breathed deeply.

'So what are you doing out here, Deputy?' Ivy demanded. 'I reckoned you'd be kept busy around town for a couple of days.'

'I came to check on the posse I sent out after you,' Kennett said slowly.

'Yeah, sure. We laid for them — had to teach them some respect.' Ivy laughed. 'They hung back after that. So where are they now, and how come you rode in here? Did someone in town tell you where to look for me?'

'How could anyone in town know where you are?' Kennett asked, wondering who could be in cahoots with a bunch of outlaws.

'Don't ask questions. Was Jake Blundell laid low?'

'How'd you know about Blundell being shot?' Kennett demanded.

'I set it up. Blundell got too big for his boots. When he took over Circle B he figured he could turn his back on his old pards, and I reckoned he needed a lesson.'

'Mack Forster shot Blundell,' Lew mused. 'Was it on your say-so?'

'I warned you about asking questions.' Ivy stepped closer to Kennett and swung his right fist. His knuckles caught Kennett on the left side of his face and his senses gyrated.

'Let me kill him,' Sim Walton snarled. 'He put a slug in me.'

'I'll gut-shoot you if you don't butt out,' Ivy growled.

Kennett leaned his right elbow on the table and lowered his chin into his cupped hand, struggling to retain his wavering senses. There were dark spots before his eyes and a roaring sound in his ears. He half-closed his eyes against the lamplight and looked around the cabin. Sim Walton was standing in the background, a bloodstained bandage around his wounded shoulder. He was holding a pistol that was pointed at Kennett's head, and there was an eager expression on his face that reminded

Kennett of a hungry dog looking at red meat.

He tried to bring his mind back under control. There were so many questions demanding answers, and the little he was learning from Hap Ivy only served to baffle rather than ease him. There was so much going on in town that he knew nothing about. He breathed deeply, forcing his mind to concentrate on what was happening, but a cold thought lay underneath all the uncertainty. He was in a tight spot, and at the moment there seemed to be no way out. He was a prisoner of a bunch of callous killers, and sensed that they would ultimately kill him.

7

Hap Ivy stood over Kennett, his right hand grasping the butt of his holstered gun. Sim Walton was grinning maliciously, the desire to kill shining clear and bright in his eyes. Kennett gritted his teeth and remained silent. Ivy relaxed and moved away, his gaze remaining on Kennett, an expression on his face that warned Kennett that he was facing death. But the danger moment passed and Ivy relaxed.

'Rafferty,' Ivy said, 'take this smart lawman out to the barn and hogtie him. I'll talk to him again in the morning, before I let Walton finish him off. You go with them, Portree, and make sure Kennett is tied properly. I want him guarded through the night. You and Rafferty can spell each other. Now get him out of here. Mrs Piercey, let's have some grub, and make it quick.'

Rafferty drew his gun and motioned for Kennett to get to his feet. He stuck the muzzle of the pistol under Kennett's nose.

'You heard the man,' he said. 'Out to the barn, and don't try anything or you won't live to see the sun come up.'

Kennett dragged himself to his feet and walked to the door, followed by Rafferty and Portree. They left the cabin and went into the barn, with Rafferty's gun muzzle prodding Kennett's spine every step of the way.

Portree struck a match and looked around for a lantern. He found one and lit it.

'Find a rope and bind him,' Rafferty said.

Portree obeyed, and Kennett protested when the rope was pulled tightly over his injured left arm. Portree struck him across the face and continued roping him, then tripped him so that he fell into a pile of straw.

'I don't wanta hear anything else outa you until the sun shines,' Rafferty said. 'I'll take the first watch, Portree. Come and relieve me at midnight.'

Portree nodded and departed. Rafferty moved out of Kennett's reach and settled down on a pile of straw. He placed his pistol by his side and soon began to snore. Kennett spent some minutes trying to get free of the restraining rope, but his left arm was useless, too painful to move, and he was unable to make any impression on the knots. His head was aching, his wounds were sore, and his mind was vibrant with the knowledge that he would probably be killed in the morning.

His thoughts meandered through gaps in his memory as he tried to grasp what had happened in town. Ivy had been aware of some of the incidents that had occurred, and the outlaw's mention of Jake Blundell's shooting hinted at some unsuspected gang sympathizer being at large in the community. Ivy also said that Jake Blundell had been known to him for years. Did that mean that Blundell had once been a member of the gang?

Kennett shook his head at the thought, although he had no idea of Blundell's earlier life. As far as he knew, Sarah's uncle had always been at Circle B, running the place to Sarah's advantage. Had Mack Forster been in cahoots with Ivy? The gang boss seemed to have had prior knowledge of Forster's attempt on Blundell's life. Kennett sighed when his ignorance of past events prevented him from making any kind of judgement on the situation around Black Horse Creek. He tried to block his thoughts but they hammered mercilessly in a vicious circle until he was sorely tried by his efforts to make sense of what had occurred and tried vainly to rest.

A furtive sound at the door of the barn attracted his attention and he raised his head to peer through the gloom. The door was closed. The sound of Rafferty's snoring rasped through the natural silence. Kennett kept his gaze on the door, expecting to see one of the gang appear. The door opened slowly and noiselessly, and then a dark figure crossed the threshold. Lamplight glinted on a pistol in the man's hand. Kennett caught his breath. This was not a member of the gang.

The man came across to where Rafferty was snoring. His Stetson was shadowing his face, and Kennett had no opportunity to identify him. He watched intently, his breath catching in his throat when the newcomer bent over the sleeping outlaw and slammed the barrel of his gun against Rafferty's head. Rafferty jerked and then subsided. The newcomer turned and came to Kennett, and lamplight shone fully on his face, revealing the grim features of Lin Cooper, brother of Thad Cooper, the murdered town marshal.

Cooper grinned tensely at Kennett and untied him.

'I've been watching this place since before sundown,' he told Kennett. 'I caught up with the gang and fell in behind them. I wanted to find their hideout before coming for you and a posse, but they stopped off here and looked like staying for a spell. When you showed up I hung around looking for a chance to get to you.' He helped Kennett to his feet. 'We can hit this bunch now. We'll be more than a match for them. I'll hogtie this one and then we'll go into the cabin and take the others.'

'I was wondering what had become of you,' Kennett said. 'Hogtie Rafferty. I'll take his gun.'

Kennett felt easier with Rafferty's pistol in his hand. He checked the weapon while Cooper tied the outlaw. Cooper was grinning.

'I'm gonna enjoy this,' he said, and kicked Rafferty in the ribs after tying a last knot in the rope. 'We'll walk straight into the cabin and catch them cold, huh?'

'I won't argue with that,' Kennett responded. 'Just bear in mind that I want this gang alive. I have some questions that need answers, and Ivy is the man with all the knowledge.'

'I'm your man,' Cooper retorted. 'Let's go get 'em.'

He led the way out of the barn and around to the front of the cabin. There was a window to the left of the cabin door and Kennett peered through the undraped glass. Ivy, Portree and Walton were seated at the table inside, eating food that had been prepared for them. Piercey was seated by the stove. His wife was busy washing pots and pans at a sink to the rear of the cabin.

Kennett paused only to give last instructions to Cooper.

'I'll enter first and move to the left. You come in and go to the right. Don't shoot unless you have to.'

'There'll be shooting,' Cooper replied. 'This whole bunch is hair-triggered.'

Kennett drew a deep breath and went to the door. He paused for a moment and then kicked the door wide and lunged into the cabin. His gun was levelled at the outlaws as he stepped to the left, and Cooper entered hard on his heels and slid to the right. Their abrupt entrance caused the gang to freeze momentarily. Hap Ivy looked up, and raised his hands instantly. Walton did not move, his face expressing shock. Portree's head jerked around and he reached instinctively for his holstered gun.

Kennett shouted a warning against movement but Portree was single-minded. He clawed at his pistol and jerked it clear of the holster. Cooper fired instantly, filling the cabin with thunder. Portree jerked, twisted, and fell off his chair. He lay huddled on the floor and blood trickled from a hole in his chest.

Cooper went forward and disarmed Ivy and Walton. Piercey got up and produced a rope. He bound both outlaws. Kennett bent over Portree, who was dead.

'Do you need food?' asked Mrs Piercey. She was a tall, hard-faced woman, grey-haired, her eyes alert and untroubled as she looked at Kennett.

'Thank you,' Kennett responded.

'We'd better eat before we set out for town. Cooper, fetch Rafferty in from the barn and we'll keep a sharp eye on this bunch.'

'I reckon you saved our lives,' Piercey said when he had finished binding Ivy and Walton. 'They said they wouldn't leave us alive when they rode out in the morning. I thought our last hours had come.'

Kennett was content. He stayed long enough for food, and then set out for Black Horse Creek with his prisoners. Portree was slung across the back of a horse. Cooper rode at the rear of the party.

* * *

It was well past midnight when they reached Black Horse Creek. No lights showed anywhere except in the window of the law office. Kennett looked around anxiously as they reined up and dismounted. He stood by, favouring his left arm, while Cooper dragged the

174

three outlaws out of their saddles and marched them into the office. Frank Casper unlocked a cell and the prisoners were pushed inside. Cooper holstered his pistol as soon as the cell door was locked.

'I need some sleep now,' he said. 'Can I hit the sack in here? It's too late to find a place in town.'

'Sure.' Kennett nodded. 'There's a room out back by the kitchen where you can get your head down. Show him, Frank, and then attend to the horses while I write a report about capturing the gang.'

He sat down at the desk, but after attempting unsuccessfully to write the report he leaned back in the chair and surrendered to his tiredness. He fell asleep despite the pain in his left arm, and did not stir until the sun came up. When he straightened in the chair he saw Frank Casper lounging on a chair by the desk. The jailer grinned when Kennett lurched to his feet and stretched to get rid of the kinks in his limbs and neck.

'How are you feeling this morning, Lew? You looked like death when you walked in last night. It was a hard day, huh?'

'One of the worst I've had in this job,' Kennett admitted. 'And it could get worse today. I'll have to get word to Sheriff Dobey about the situation, and he might send me some help. There is more than enough going on around here for a couple of extra deputies, but Dobey thinks I can cope.'

'Mrs Allen came in last night to talk about Joe,' said Casper. 'She wanted me to release him. I told her I'm only the jailer around here and I got no say in the comings and goings. She's coming to see you this morning.'

'I've got a lot on my plate today.' Kennett shook his head. 'And I don't know where to start.'

'I can stay on duty as long as you need me,' Casper offered. 'Tom Eke will come on duty at eight. Perhaps you'll need the both of us around now you've got extra prisoners.'

'You're right. I can't handle the Ivy gang and check out what happened in town yesterday.' Kennett went through to the cell by the back kitchen and found Lin Cooper stirring. 'I'm going for breakfast,' he said. 'Come along. I want to talk to you.'

They left the office and walked along the street to the diner.

'What are your plans?' Kennett asked.

'I came here to spend some time with Thad,' Cooper replied. 'But his death changes everything.'

'How do you feel about taking over his job?'

'What, step into my dead brother's boots?' Cooper laughed mirthlessly.

'It'll give you something to occupy your mind until you decide what you want to do. Frank Fallon is the mayor, and he owns the hotel. When I told him Thad was dead he suggested you as his replacement.'

'I'll think about it.' Cooper sighed. 'I

was a deputy sheriff in Dodge City for six months, but Wyatt Earp and his brothers cleaned up so I pulled out.'

'Dodge was mighty tough, by all accounts,' Kennett observed.

'Everywhere is tough when you're wearing a law badge,' Cooper retorted.

Mrs Allen served Kennett's breakfast, and then inquired about her son. She looked worried, her movements quick and nervous.

'I didn't get the chance to talk to him this morning,' Kennett replied. 'Will you get in touch with the jailer? There'll be some food needed at the jail. We picked up some bad men last night.'

'I'll go along there shortly,' she replied. 'Can't you let Joe out of jail?'

'How would you feel if I let him out and someone shot him, or he was lynched?'

Her face paled at his words, and she shook her head.

Kennett felt better with a good breakfast under his belt. He left Cooper finishing his meal and went along to the hotel, wanting to talk to Sarah about Jake Blundell. Sarah was in the hotel dining room, merely picking at her breakfast. Her lovely face was pale and wore a harsh expression. She sighed when she looked up and saw Kennett, and he sat down opposite her.

'You don't seem very pleased to see me, Sarah,' he said.

'I've got a lot on my mind,' she replied in a low tone.

'I know. I've been watching you lately, and I'd like to know what's troubling you. Talk to me! Tell me what's on your mind. I might be able to help you. And if you can't confide in me then you can't talk to anyone.'

'I can't tell you anything,' she declared.

'Why? Is it because I'm a deputy?' He paused, and when she did not reply he sighed impatiently. 'If you won't talk to me because I am a deputy then your problem must be something that's crooked.'

'I don't know what you mean.' Her

tone filled with anger. 'Do you think I'm mixed up in a crooked business?'

Kennett put his right hand over her left hand and squeezed it reassuringly. 'Come on, Sarah. You can confide in me. I know there's something wrong, and the only way you'll get over it is by telling me what it is.'

He paused and waited for a reply. She shook her head and rose from the table, leaving her breakfast almost untouched.

'I have to go and check up on Uncle Jake,' she said quickly.

Kennett reached out and grasped her arm as she passed him. He pulled her to a standstill and pushed her gently into the chair beside him. She made an effort to regain her feet but he held her and she subsided.

'Jake is in good hands. You can spare me a few moments. I have to talk to you, Sarah. I caught the Ivy gang last night and now they're in jail. Hap Ivy said some things about Jake that set me thinking, and I need to ask questions.

Your dad has been dead about five years, you said, and Jake took over the running of the Circle B at that time. When I came on the scene three years ago I thought Jake had been a partner in the business with your father, but you said yesterday that Jake was merely running the ranch for you. So how long has Jake been at the ranch? And where was he before he took over from your dad?'

'What did Ivy tell you about Jake?' Sarah countered.

'Just answer the questions,' he replied.

She sighed. 'I don't see how this can help you, but if that's what you want to know then I'll tell you. We never saw Jake for years. He just turned up at the ranch about a month after my dad died. I had no idea how to handle the ranch and he seemed to know all about the business so he took over, and he's done a real good job.'

'What was he doing before he showed up here?'

'I don't know. He never said, and I

had no reason to ask him.'

'So what's worrying you? Has it got to do with Jake? Or is it me you're concerned about?'

'Don't ask me, Lew.' She shook her head. 'I don't know what's going on so I can't tell you anything.'

'You must tell me what's on your mind,' he insisted. 'What area of your life is bugging you?'

'It's not you,' she said instantly. 'Please don't think that.'

'That's a relief.' He smiled, trying to make light of the situation, but there was no reaction from her. He heard her sigh, and his impatience flared. 'I'm trying to solve a whole bunch of problems right now,' he said sharply, 'and whatever is bothering you could involve one of them. That's why I insist you talk to me. Come on, Sarah. If you care anything at all about me then you'll want to make my job easier. So why have you clammed up?'

'It's to do with the ranch,' she said hesitantly.

'So what's worrying you?'

'I'm not happy with some of the crew Uncle Jake has hired.'

'Give me details.'

'Bull Hamner and the four men he rides with. They were hired to protect the ranch from rustlers, but Hamner acts more like a bad man. Uncle Jake doesn't seem to have any control over him. In fact, you'd think Hamner was the boss, not Uncle Jake.'

'There has to be more to it than that. Keep talking.'

'Hamner frightens me. He waylays me around the ranch every chance he gets and his talk is wild. He's made threats against my uncle. And now Jake has been shot I suspect Hamner arranged it.'

'I can soon get to the bottom of that,' Kennett said, starting to his feet. 'I've talked to Hamner and I don't like him. He's a bad man, and I need an excuse to pick him. What you've just told me will do very nicely.'

'Don't go after him, Lew.' Sarah

grasped his hand and gripped it tightly. 'He's got some kind of a hold on Uncle Jake, and he's threatened to ruin us if I go against him. I think he's one of the Ivy gang.'

'That's what I need to know.' Kennett pulled his hand from her grasp. 'Stick around the hotel until you hear from me again. I've been looking for a way to break the deadlock that seems to exist around here and Bull Hamner could be the lever.'

He went to the door despite Sarah's protests. He stepped out to the sidewalk and was startled by the crash of shooting that tore through the silence and echoed across the town. When he realized that the disturbance was coming from the direction of the law office he started running in that direction. He could see several horses standing outside the office, and figures were moving around in the swirling gun smoke that was drifting across the street. He drew his gun and hastened to join the action.

8

Three men were standing in the street in front of the law office, and were holding several horses by their reins. They were shooting in Kennett's direction. A bullet whined past his head and another slammed into a post he was passing. He realized that the shooting was intended to deter townsmen from approaching the office and increased his speed. The door of the law office was opened and a group of men emerged, holding guns. They ran to the horses and mounted. Kennett recognized the diminutive figure of Hap Ivy and the massive shape of Bull Hamner among them. He triggered his pistol.

The shooting rapidly increased in volume. Kennett stepped sideways into a doorway. A man came up from his right and joined him. It was Lin Cooper, who was holding both his guns. Kennett moved out to the sidewalk and Cooper joined him. They went on towards the law office with guns firing. Gun smoke drifted. Riders were moving away from the law office. Kennett paused and aimed his shots carefully although he was trembling with excitement. He picked Hap Ivy as a target, determined that the outlaw would not escape. His second shot struck the diminutive outlaw. Ivy jerked and slipped sideways out of his saddle.

Cooper was running along the street, firing his guns alternately. Kennett kept abreast of him. Slugs crackled along the street. The knot of men at the law office was scattering. Two went down in the dust and the rest climbed into their saddles and made tracks.

Kennett fired until his hammer clicked on a spent cartridge. He halted to reload, sweating and breathless. The riders were heading out of town. Cooper halted and set his feet. His twin guns blazed. Saddles emptied. Kennett finished reloading, lifted his gun, and saw no more targets. Several horses were galloping out of gunshot range, their riders now huddled in the dust. Ahead of them, four riders were escaping on the trail south. Hamner was one of them and so was Rafferty. But Hap Ivy lay crumpled in the street where he had fallen.

Cooper paused and reloaded his guns, plucking fresh shells from the loops on his cartridge belts. He was grinning, looking over the small battlefield with satisfaction on his sweating face.

'I'll fetch our horses from the barn,' he rapped. 'We'll take out after those who got away, huh?'

'Sure thing,' Kennett replied without hesitation. 'I'll check the men we downed and tidy up around here until you get back.'

Cooper hastened away along the street and Kennett went to the scene of the shooting. His pistol was steady in his hand. He came across one of the men who had accompanied Bull Hamner at the Forster cabin, stretched out dead, and Sim Walton was lying on his face, also dead, his blood dribbling into the dust. Kennett checked another of Hamner's associates, who was breathing his last, and then came upon Hap Ivy. The outlaw was on his face, but still breathing. There was a splotch of blood on his right shoulder blade.

Kennett turned Ivy over. The outlaw was unconscious. Kennett removed a gun from Ivy's holster. There was a big exit wound in Ivy's shoulder. He had been dusted both sides. Kennett straightened and looked around, then moved to a wounded horse, examined it, and put it out of its misery. Townsmen were appearing on the street and came crowding around.

'Two of you bring Ivy into the office,' Kennett ordered, and stepped on to the sidewalk. He looked around, his eyes filled with anger. It was time he cut down on the lawlessness that held the town in its grip, and he vowed that this would be the last time outlaws walked with impunity along Main Street. He entered the law office.

The office was empty except for the motionless body of Frank Casper, who was lying dead beside the desk, still clutching a pistol. Kennett went into the cell block, paused in the doorway and looked around. He was surprised to see Goymer and Downey still in their cell, and Mike Attew, the butcher, was on the bunk in his cell, apparently asleep. Joe Allen was sitting on his bunk, although his cell door was unlocked. He had made no attempt to escape. Kennett ignored the two Circle B men and confronted Allen, who got to his feet and came to the cell door.

'What happened in here, Joe?' Kennett demanded.

'I don't really know, Lew,' the youngster replied.

'You were here! What did you see?'

'The jailer came in with a man who was holding a gun. The jailer was forced to turn the outlaws loose. He unlocked my door but I stayed put. They went back into the office, and then a whole lot of shooting started outside. That's all I can tell you.'

Kennett stood thinking. Then he made a decision. 'OK, Joe, you can get out of here and go home to your mother. If I were you I wouldn't stray too far from the diner in the next few days. I'm gonna keep Goymer and Downey penned up in here, so they won't bother you. Go on, beat it, and don't get into any trouble.'

'I sure won't, Lew.' Allen brushed past Kennett and hurried out of the cell block.

Kennett went back into the front office and sat down at the desk. He looked at the body of Frank Casper and his anger rose in his chest, threatening to choke him. It was time to start cleaning up, he thought, and he knew where he had to begin.

Hap Ivy was carried into the office.

'Put him in a cell,' Kennett ordered, and picked up the bunch of keys.

Ivy was carried into the cell block, and Kennett felt a twinge of satisfaction as he locked a cell door on him. The man would not get a second chance at escaping! He told one of the townsmen to fetch the doctor.

He heard the sound of hoofs in the street when he returned to the front office, and went to the door. Noah Leake, the liveryman, stepped down from Kennett's horse and held out the reins.

'I saw that bunch come in here and guessed you'd want your horse, Lew,' Leake said.

'Thanks, Noah.' Kennett nodded. He wrapped the reins around a hitching pole. 'I'll be riding out shortly. But I've got the boss outlaw still in jail, and the rest of the gang will have to wait until I can get around to them. I've got some problems to sort out in town, and they won't wait.'

Lin Cooper rode along the street and reined up beside Kennett but did not dismount.

'Are you ready to ride?' Cooper demanded.

'I can't leave right now,' Kennett replied.

'Then I'll see you later. I'm heading out after the gang.'

Cooper spurred his horse and departed in a cloud of dust. Kennett watched him. He shook his head, and was about to enter the office when a voice hailed him and he turned to see Ossie Noble, the undertaker, coming along the sidewalk.

'Looks like you've given me a full day's work,' Noble observed, glancing at the bodies in the street. 'Any locals killed?'

'No. There are only strangers out here. But Frank Casper is dead in the office. Get this buzzard bait off the street as soon as you can, Ossie.'

The undertaker turned and departed hurriedly. Doc Mitchell emerged from his house, carrying a medical bag, and Kennett waited for him to arrive.

'I've got Hap Ivy back in a cell and he needs attention, Doc.'

They entered the office and Mitchell went to check on the outlaw. He returned after some minutes.

'I've stopped the bleeding but I need to have him over in my office to treat him,' Mitchell said. 'Would you arrange for some men to carry him over, Lew?'

'Sure. How is Jake Blundell this morning?'

'He's comfortable in a room at the hotel. Sarah wanted him there. She's with him.'

'I saw her at the hotel earlier. I'm going to talk to Jake now.'

'He should be OK this morning,' Mitchell observed.

The doctor left. Tom Eke, the relief jailer, entered the office, and halted in shock when he saw Frank Casper dead on the floor.

'Jeez!' he ejaculated. 'Who in hell killed Frank?'

'I don't know yet, but I mean to find out,' Kennett said. 'Can you take over here for a spell? I've got some work to do. I should be out chasing my escaped prisoners but I can't get away from here yet.'

'Sure.' Eke, a short, fleshy man with a

round face and hard blue eyes, walked to the desk and sat down. 'You do what you have to, Lew. I'll hold the fort.'

'I've spoken to Ossie Noble. He'll clean up the street and remove Frank. I'd better cut along and tell Frank's wife what's happened. Hap Ivy is still behind bars and Goymer and Downey of the Circle B are in a cell. So is Mike Attew. They're not to be released unless I say so.'

'Attew?' Eke grimaced. 'Has he been on another drunk?'

'Not this time. I've got him on suspicion of buying rustled beeves, and he tried to carve me up when I went to arrest him.'

Eke whistled through his teeth. 'The hell you say! But now that you mention it, I've been wondering about Attew for a long time.'

'What makes you say that?' Kennett looked up from checking his pistol.

'I live on the back lots near the timber yard, and I've seen cattle being driven into the slaughterhouse. It was mainly the men who drive the cattle that caught my attention. There were some real hard cases among them.'

'Did you see anyone you know?' Kennett asked.

'Sure. Mack Forster did a lot of business with Attew.'

'Do you know Forster was killed earlier?'

'I heard about it as I came along the street. You killed him, huh?'

'I saw him come out of the butcher's alley and shoot Jake Blundell.' Kennett explained the incident.

'I happened to look out my window earlier when Forster was leaving the timber yard.' Eke frowned. 'He went into the slaughterhouse for a few minutes, and when he came out he was carrying a rifle. He went into the alley that leads to the street. And you say he shot Jake Blundell?'

'Yeah. I happened to be standing in front of the store and saw Forster coming out of the alley. I thought he was aiming at me when he fired, but

Jake Blundell was sitting his horse in front of the bank, talking to John Busby, and he fell off his horse with a bullet in him. Didn't you hear the shooting?'

'No. I never hear much from inside the house.'

'Did you see anyone else at the rear end of that alley after Forster entered it?'

'No. My wife had a meal ready for me and I went into the back kitchen for it.'

Kennett thought about the second bullet that had hit Mack Forster. It could only have been fired from the timber yard end of the alley. And what had happened to the rifle Forster used? It had been lying in the alley immediately after the shooting, and it seemed obvious that Mike Attew had given it to Forster — but it had disappeared by the time Kennett had returned to the alley, having checked on Blundell along the street. Had Attew collected it from the alley after the shooting?'

'I'll leave you to it, Tom,' he said. 'I'd better get moving. I'll talk to Attew later.'

He left the office and went along to the hotel. He asked at the desk for Sarah's room and ascended the stairs to the first floor. She answered the door when he knocked, and gazed at him with fear in her eyes.

'That shooting,' she gasped. 'Were you involved?'

'Yeah, and you can forget about Hamner and his threats,' Lew replied.

'Why? What's happened?'

'There was a jailbreak, and Hamner was one of the men involved. He got away with some of the Ivy gang, but I shot Hap Ivy out of his saddle and he's back behind bars. How is Jake this morning? I need to talk to him before I do anything else.'

'He's awake, but he's not feeling good.' She emerged from the room and closed the door. 'There's no need to bother him right now, Lew. Let him rest. In view of what's happened I'll tell you a little more about my worries.'

'I'm listening.' Kennett leaned against the wall beside the door and removed his hat to wipe his forehead.

'Just after Hamner and his men showed up at the ranch a few weeks ago I told Jake what was bothering me and he said that he'd been in an outlaw gang run by Hamner. He left the gang when he heard that my father had died, and came to take over the ranch. It gave him a chance of getting away from his old life, and everything was going along all right until Hamner showed up. Hamner is one of Hap Ivy's gang, and Ivy sent him and the other four men to threaten Uncle Jake with exposure if he didn't help the gang to clean out this range of cattle. Ivy also means to rob John Busby's bank before finally pulling out.'

Kennett straightened and put on his hat. His eyes were narrowed as he studied Sarah's anxious face.

'I wish you'd told me this earlier,' he said. 'It would have prevented the death of several good men.'

'Jake has done nothing wrong since he arrived at Circle B,' Sarah said defensively. 'He sold some stock to Forster, and the deals are entered in the ranch accounts. When the rustling started he soon worked out what was going on and said Forster was responsible.'

'I get the picture,' Kennett said.

'What will you do?' She seemed strained almost to breaking point.

'I'll pick up Hamner and everyone connected with the business. Then it will all come out in the wash.'

'What about Uncle Jake? He's done nothing wrong around here, and he's been trying to put his past behind him.'

'We'll see what comes to light when I get my hands on Hamner,' Kennett replied. 'I'd better get moving. Sit tight here and stay close to the hotel, huh?'

He had plenty to think about as he left the hotel, but did not have sufficient knowledge to put two and two together. He stood on the sidewalk and looked around the street. It always amazed him that folk could go about their normal everyday lives and apparently see nothing of the undercurrents, however evil and crooked, that existed in the community. He wondered about the unknown person who was making a career of stealing from his neighbours, and was concerned that he could not even begin to locate him.

But the riddle of the missing rifle was uppermost in his mind. The time lapse surrounding the shooting of Jake Blundell was narrow, and he walked slowly along to the alley beside the slaughterhouse, making for the far end. The rifle had been lying just inside the alley when he reached it after the ambush. He remembered seeing it. He had ignored it at the time because he had been concentrating on Forster, who had at that moment been lying almost at the far end of the alley. So someone had removed the rifle from the alley after he had left Forster to check on Jake Blundell lying outside the bank.

Kennett frowned. It was obvious that Attew, having given the rifle to Forster before the shooting, would want it back afterwards to conceal its existence. But Forster, hit by Kennett's first shot, had dropped it. Had Attew then killed Forster for fear that he would talk about the shooting when arrested? That seemed a logical conclusion.

He moved to the far end of the alley and looked out over the back lots. He could see Hungate moving around his timber yard, and wondered if he was involved in the shooting. He entered the slaughterhouse and looked around, checked out the big room where slaughtered steers were stored, and then went along a passage that led to the rear of the shop fronting Main Street. He stopped at the door that led into the alley, unlocked it, and stepped outside. He was only thirty yards from the street end of the alley, and he could see how easy it would have been for Attew to have recovered the rifle from where Forster had dropped it.

He went back into the building by the side door, locked it, and moved on towards the rear of the shop. There were several doors on the left side of the passage that gave access to various storerooms, and he checked through them, looking for the rifle. He found nothing until he opened the last door on the left and peered in, and was shocked to find Joe Allen sitting at a table inside, busily cleaning a rifle.

Allen dropped the rifle and sprang to his feet when the door opened. Kennett quickly recovered from his surprise.

'What are you doing here, Joe?' he demanded, the fingers of his right hand clenched around the butt of his holstered pistol.

'Mike Attew asked me to come in, Lew.' Allen was badly shaken. He was trembling, his voice shaky and his face pale. 'When I was in the next cell to him he said he'd pay me if I was released before him to come and do this job.'

'I reckon this rifle is the one used by Mack Forster to shoot Jake Blundell,'

Kennett said, 'and you're getting rid of the evidence that it has been fired recently.'

'I don't know anything about that, Lew. I'm only doing a favour for Attew. He told me the rifle was in the cupboard here, and asked me to do a good job on it.'

Kennett picked up the rifle and examined it. It had been cleaned and oiled thoroughly and looked as if it had not been fired recently.

'You've done a good job on it,' Kennett observed. 'And if Attew asked you to clean it then it must have been real dirty, huh?'

'Yeah, it was fired earlier today. Mr Attew said he's bothered by rats that get in after meat. I said I'd come in and check, and shoot a few rats for him while he's stuck behind bars.'

Kennett studied Allen's face, not knowing whether to accept his story. But he now had the rifle and proof that it had been fired recently — Allen's statement would corroborate that. Also

Attew might admit his culpability when confronted with the fact that Joe Allen had been caught in the act of cleaning the weapon.

'Am I in trouble, Lew?' Allen demanded.

'I don't know yet. You're surely making things difficult for yourself, coming in here knowing Attew is in jail. You should have turned him down flat. I'll want a statement from you about what you were doing in here and why.'

'Sure, Lew, I've got nothing to hide.'

'OK, so beat it now and don't talk to anyone about this. I'll come to the diner later and get a statement from you.'

Allen departed quickly. Kennett picked up the rifle. He stood thinking deeply for some moments, and then picked up a cartridge from the half-dozen lying on the table and thumbed it into the rifle. He went back to the slaughtering area and fired a shot into the carcass of a steer which had been slaughtered. He took the rifle with him when he returned to the jail.

Attew was awake when Kennett

entered the cell block and confronted him. The butcher was stretched out on the bunk with a hand to his head.

'I found this rifle in a storeroom in the slaughterhouse,' Kennett said casually. 'It's been fired recently, and I suspect it's the weapon Mack Forster used to shoot Jake Blundell. Charlie Hungate said Forster left the timber yard without a rifle so it's fairly obvious he borrowed this from you, and you took it back off him after he shot Blundell with it. Also, I have a witness who saw Forster enter the slaughter-house without a rifle and leave within a minute or so carrying one. Why did you give Forster this rifle?'

'What in hell are you talking about?' Attew said. 'I don't own a rifle. Just leave me alone. I've got a bad head.'

'You're lying, Attew. You asked Joe Allen to go to your premises and clean the rifle. I caught him in the slaughter-house and he admitted it.'

'Did he tell you that?'

'I caught him red-handed. You'd

better start telling the truth. I know you've had dealings with Forster, and I wanta know why you wanted Jake Blundell dead and helped Forster in the crime. I have evidence that Forster bought cattle off Blundell and sold them on to you. On the face of it they were bought legally, but I suspect they were stolen, and Blundell probably got a rake-off. I'll take a statement off you shortly, and I'll be interested to learn why you attacked me for no apparent reason if you're not guilty as hell. I'm gonna prove it. So why don't you come clean and admit it?'

'I can't think straight right now,' Attew replied, holding his head in both hands. 'I'll talk tomorrow. Give me a break and let me get some shuteye. I'll give you the lowdown tomorrow.'

Kennett turned away, aware that he would get nothing more at that moment. He went back into the front office and sat down to write a report on events to date, aware that he was at last seeing light at the end of the tunnel.

9

Kennett did not get far with his report; he barely started writing when he heard horses out in the street. He looked up when the front door opened, and sprang to his feet when Asa McCall and Lenny Dawson, the remaining two members of the posse, entered. They were travel-stained and weary. McCall, an older man, was weather-beaten and slow-moving. His face showed fatigue. He dropped into the chair beside the desk and slumped forward, hanging his head until his chin rested on his chest. Lenny Dawson was much younger, in his twenties, short and black-haired. He sat down on a corner of the desk and looked at Kennett with unblinking brown eyes that carried more than a hint of exhaustion.

'We followed tracks until sundown, Lew,' Dawson said, 'and then camped for the night and went on again this morning. We finished up in Piercey's yard, and he told us what happened last night. So you finally caught the gang, huh?'

'I'm glad you got back in one piece,' Kennett observed, and told them about the subsequent jailbreak.

McCall sprang to his feet. 'We'll get fresh horses and go out again,' he said sharply.

'Hold it,' Kennett rapped. 'With Hap Ivy in the jail there's no gang left to speak of, and Ivy won't get the chance to escape again. I'm trying to sort out a load of trouble that's blown up here in town, and that's at the top of my list. You two go and get some food and rest up. If I take to the trail it won't be for a few days, and then I'll need all the help I can get.'

Dawson nodded and turned away immediately. He paused in the doorway and looked back at McCall.

'I'll take your nag along to the stable, Asa, while you go into the diner and order some chuck. I'm plumb tuckered out, and you must be almost on your knees.'

McCall lifted a hand in acknowledgement and Dawson left the office.

'I'm getting too old for this sort of thing,' McCall said wearily. 'But I'll ride with you if you do go out after the rest of that crooked bunch, Lew. Who busted them out of jail, anyway? Have you got any idea?'

'Yeah, and I'll be looking him up pretty soon.' Kennett paused, and then nodded. 'That reminds me of another little chore I've got to handle. You'd better get moving, Asa.'

McCall lurched to his feet and went to the door. Kennett shook his head as the posse man departed. He heaved a sigh, picked up the cell keys, and then went into the cell block. He paused at the door of the cell holding Downey and Goymer. Downey, his shoulder heavily bandaged, was propped up on his bunk. He glared at Kennett but remained silent.

'When are you gonna turn me loose?'

209

Pete Goymer demanded. 'I ain't broken the law. I hit that townsman in self-defence.'

'It seems everyone I put behind bars is innocent,' Kennett replied. 'I suppose you're gonna say you didn't pull a gun on me, Downey, huh?'

'I wasn't gonna shoot you, for Chris'sakes!' Downey snarled. 'We brought Joe Allen into town on Blundell's say-so. Allen was on our range, and I admit that we were having some fun with him which went wrong.'

'Did Allen shoot Murphy deliberately?' Kennett demanded.

'No,' Goymer said. 'Murphy pulled his gun and Allen grabbed for it and it went off. The slug was not aimed. Allen forced the gun downwards and the slug hit Murphy.'

'So what was going on when I rode into town and saw a crowd of men shouting for a lynching?'

'We pushed the joke too far, I guess.' Downey suppressed a groan as he shifted his position on the bunk. 'And I got a slug in the shoulder!'

'Is it true Blundell has been shot?' Goymer demanded.

'Frank Casper told us,' Downey cut in.

'Mack Forster shot him,' Kennett replied. 'His life is not in danger. What can you tell me about the situation at Circle B with Forster and Hamner?'

'Forster was a crook, and at Circle B we all knew it.' Goymer shrugged. 'Hamner had nothing to do with us. He's an outlaw, and we don't mix with men like him.'

'But you didn't come into town and report him to the law,' Kennett mused. 'And he's working for Jake Blundell, huh?'

'We didn't like him being around and were gonna take care of that problem ourselves, when we got the word from Blundell,' Downey said. 'The boss didn't want Hamner around. But you can't do much when a gang of outlaws move in. Did you know Hamner is working with Hap Ivy?'

Kennett suppressed a sigh. 'It's got so I don't know who is doing what any more,' he said. 'I'm gonna hold you two until I can get around to checking out your story about what happened with Joe Allen. I'll talk to Blundell, and if his story tallies with yours I'll spring you out of here.'

He went back into the front office as the street door opened. Mrs Allen stepped across the threshold, with Tom Eke, the jailer, behind her.

'I went along to the diner to order breakfast for the prisoners, Lew,' Eke said.

'I need to talk to you, Lew,' Mrs Allen cut in. 'I'm worried about Joe. He came into the diner a few minutes ago and said you'd caught him in the slaughterhouse doing a job for Mike Attew, and he's afraid he's broken the law. Is he in more trouble?'

'As far as I know Joe ain't in any trouble with the law,' Kennett said. 'Sure I found him in the slaughterhouse. But all I'll want from him is a statement about what he was doing in there. I reckon he's been a mite foolish, but he won't be jailed for that.'

'Thank you for being so understanding.' Mrs Allen seemed to be on the point of breaking down.

Kennett reached out and patted her shoulder. 'Don't worry about it. Joe just got caught up in some trouble, that's all. You sort out breakfast for the prisoners. I have to get moving. Tom, stick around here until I get back. I'm leaving town on a manhunt. Send word to John Carter to relieve you when you want to go off duty.'

'Sure thing, Lew! Leave this to me.'

Kennett went out to the sidewalk and looked around. His thoughts were spinning around in his head like a waterwheel in a fast current. Mrs Allen came out of the office and paused by his side.

'There's something I have to tell you, Lew,' she said hesitantly.

He gazed at her for a moment. 'About Joe?' he prompted when she remained silent, clearly struggling with a problem.

'It's been on my mind for several days, but with the trouble that came up when Joe rode out to Circle B I just didn't think the time was right to mention it to you.'

Kennett remained silent, his gaze steady on her worried face.

'Have you seen that strange-looking gun that was on display in Overman's store?' she asked at length. 'Everyone has been talking about it.'

'Reid's 'My Friend' Knuckleduster .32,' Kennett said instantly. 'Yeah, I saw it. It doesn't have a barrel, fires direct from the chambers, and can be used as a bludgeon.' He nodded. 'It's the first one I've seen.'

'I found it in Joe's bedroom when I was cleaning up.'

'Did Joe buy it?' Kennett frowned.

'When I asked him, he denied all knowledge of it.'

'Is that a fact? Ben Overman was in here earlier, talking about the store being robbed, and he mentioned the thief had taken a couple of guns. I'll check with him about the Reid's. If it was one of those the thief stole then I'll have a word with Joe. There have been several robberies about town lately.' He paused and subjected her to a searching look, noting her uneasiness. 'Are you thinking Joe might be responsible for the robberies?'

'How else would that gun get into his bedroom if he didn't put it there?' she demanded, shaking her head. 'If he is a thief then he should be punished for it. He was brought up to be honest and God-fearing; I won't have him going off the rails. He's been getting into some bad company lately and needs a sharp lesson to straighten him out. Will you look into it, Lew?'

'Where is Joe now?'

'I left him in the diner.'

'Don't say anything to him,' Kennett decided. 'I'll drop in at the store and have a word with Ben Overman, and then see Joe.'

Mrs Allen nodded, her face showing distress. She hurried away along the sidewalk. Kennett went to the store. Ben Overman was behind the counter, serving a woman, but he looked up and grimaced at Kennett.

'Have you caught the thief yet?' he demanded.

'I'm working on it right now,' Kennett replied. 'You told me earlier that the thief stole a couple of guns, Ben. What make were they?'

'They were a couple of specials. One was a Remington Elliot .32, which has a ring instead of a trigger, with a curved, trigger-like stop behind it, and carries five shots. The other was a Reid's 'My Friend' Knuckleduster .32.'

'I remember seeing the Reid's on display,' Kennett said.

'That's right. I don't reckon there's another one in the county like it. Why are you asking about it? Have you seen it around town?'

'Like I said, I'm looking into the robberies.' Kennett turned away. 'I'll talk to you later, Ben.'

Kennett went on to the diner, and found Joe Allen cleaning tables. Allen looked up quickly at Kennett's arrival.

'Have you come for that statement, Lew?' he asked.

'Not right now. I wanta talk to you about the Reid's .32 your mother found in your bedroom.'

Allen's face changed expression, flushed to a dull red colour. He pushed his right hand under his apron, reached into his pants pocket, and pulled out the Reid's .32. Kennett, anticipating action, stepped in swiftly and grabbed Allen's gun wrist. The weapon fell out of Allen's grasp. Allen sidestepped and punched wildly at Kennett, his fist thudding against Kennett's left fore-arm. Agony flared through the knife slash in the limb. Kennett gritted his teeth and struck at Allen with his right fist.

Allen took the blow on the side of his chin. His knees crumpled and he fell to the floor on his hands and knees, shaking his head as his senses receded. Kennett picked up the Reid's pistol and stuck it into his pocket, and then drew his holstered pistol. Allen began to surge upright, clearly determined to resist. Kennett's left arm was hanging useless at his side, pain searing through the wound. A quick glance at it showed fresh blood seeping through the thick bandage.

Allen was halfway to his feet when the toe of Kennett's boot struck him in the face. He went back down on the floor. Kennett bent over him and pushed the muzzle of his gun against the youngster's left ear.

'Forget it, Joe, or I'll splatter your brains all over the diner,' he rasped. 'I reckon you'd better come with me back to the jail. You've got a lot of explaining to do, and I have some questions to ask you.'

Allen stumbled to his feet. Mrs Allen came into the diner from the back room, took in the situation at a glance, and leaned on a table for support, head hanging and her chin on her breast. Kennett could feel blood running from the knife wound in his left arm. Pain was assailing the limb in pulsating waves. He clenched his teeth and jabbed Allen's spine with the muzzle of his pistol, forcing him towards the door.

'You know where the jail is, Joe,' he said. 'Let's go.'

Several men were attracted by the sight of Kennett with his gun in hand and Allen being taken to the jail. Doc Mitchell emerged from his house as Kennett went by.

'Hey, it looks like you've started your wound bleeding, Lew,' Mitchell observed. 'I'd better take a look at it. Come into my office.'

'In a moment, Doc,' Kennett replied. 'I'll see you when I've put Joe behind bars.'

In the law office, Kennett searched Allen and then told him to sit down in front of the desk. Tom Eke stood to one side, rattling a bunch of cell keys.

'You ain't gonna put me back in a

cell, are you?' Allen demanded.

'If you've been robbing folks around town then jail is the only place for you,' said Kennett, dropping into his seat. He laid his pistol on the desk close to his right hand and took the Reid's gun from his pocket. 'So tell me about this, Joe.'

'I didn't rob anyone.'

'Where did you get this gun from?'

'It was given to me.' Allen's face was wearing a sullen expression, and he spoke hesitantly. He fell silent, shaking his head slowly.

'So who gave it to you, Joe?' Kennett kept his voice soft. 'If you didn't do the robberies then you've got nothing to fear. Just tell me how you got the gun.'

'I can't do that.' Allen looked into Kennett's eyes. 'I didn't know the gun was stolen when it was given to me, but now I do know I can't tell you who gave it.'

'Because you reckon it would be wrong to turn him in?'

'Yeah, that's right.' Allen nodded.

'If you don't talk, and I can't find out who gave the Reid's to you, it'll look like you're lying, and when you go to court to answer a charge of robbery it's gonna be hard for the judge to find you innocent. You're in a real bad hole, Joe, and your only way out of it is to come clean and tell the truth. If someone gave you the gun, knowing it was stolen, and he didn't tell you, then he's no friend, and you'd be a fool to protect him.'

'What would the judge give me if I was found guilty of stealing the gun?'

'It's not just this gun, Joe. If you are found guilty of stealing it then you'll have all the other robberies that have taken place around town thrown at you, and I reckon you'll get two years in the state prison. You wouldn't like that. I've taken a prisoner or two to that place, and it's like hell on earth. I don't think you'd survive it. So open up and tell me the truth and I'll see the blame gets pinned on the man responsible.'

Allen sat motionless and silent.

Kennett gave him time to think over the situation, but moments dragged by and Kennett became impatient.

'You can take your time thinking about this, Joe,' he said at length. 'But I've got to get my arm looked at by the doc. You can sit in a cell and decide what you wanta do. I'll come back to you later. Tom, lock him up.'

Eke jangled the cell keys. 'Come on, Joe,' he said. 'You can have the same cell again.'

Kennett watched while Allen got to his feet and walked through to the cells. Eke returned shortly, grinning.

'I reckon he'll tell you what you wanta know, Lew,' he said. 'Give him half an hour and he'll be crying for his mother.'

'I'm gonna see Doc Mitchell, Tom.' Kennett got to his feet. He slipped the Reid's .32 into his pocket, picked up his pistol from the desk and holstered it. When he left the office he went to the store.

'Sure,' Ben Overman said when

Kennett handed him the small gun. 'That's my Reid's all right. Where'd you find it?'

'I can't say at the moment. I'm still making inquiries. I'll have to keep the gun as evidence. Make a list of everything you had stolen, Ben, and I'll try to locate the items.'

He left the store and went to the doctor's house. Mitchell was in his office, and Hap Ivy was lying on the examination couch, unconscious and breathing heavily. His face was covered with a fine sheen of sweat. He was stripped to the waist, his upper body heavily bandaged.

'How is Ivy doing, Doc?' Kennett asked.

'He'll make it, barring complications,' Mitchell replied. 'He can't be moved for a couple of days.'

'He'll be safe enough,' Kennett decided. 'He's in no condition to get up and make a run for it.'

He sat down at a small table and Mitchell cut the bandage from his arm.

'You've busted some stitches,' Mitchell observed. 'You should rest up for a spell to give this a chance to heal.'

'Sure, when I've handled a couple more things,' Kennett replied.

He endured the doctor's painful ministrations and the wound was dressed. A sigh of relief escaped him when he went back to the street and headed for the hotel. Frank Fallon was inside, standing by the reception desk.

'If you're looking for Sarah you're unlucky,' Fallon said. 'She's gone out to the Circle B to get some clothes, and said to tell you she'll return later this afternoon.'

'Have you seen Jake Blundell?'

'Yeah. Sarah took me up. I'll have someone keep an eye on him until she shows up again. Blundell was lucky. He'll be up and about in a couple of weeks.'

Kennett nodded and departed. He returned to the law office. Tom Eke was sitting at the desk, and he grinned at Kennett.

'I told you Allen wouldn't hold out for long,' he said. 'When I looked in on him a few minutes ago he said he wanted to talk to you.'

Kennett went through to the cells and confronted Allen.

'What's on your mind, Joe?' he asked.

'It was Chuck Busby gave me the Reid's .32.' Allen spoke in a rush, his words seeming to tumble out of his mouth. 'He said he bought it at the store. I reckon he knew I'd get in trouble with it, and I figure he did it because he's sweet on my gal. She's been complaining about him paying her too much attention. Well, two can play at that game! I'll tell you what I know. Chuck and Brad Attew have been rustling cattle around the county, helping Mack Forster with his crooked business. Attew was spying out the range while looking for timber orders for Charlie Hungate.'

'Why did Forster shoot Jake Blundell?'

'Blundell brought in Bull Hamner and four hard cases to take over the rustling, and that put paid to Forster's business, so he decided to get even with Blundell.' Allen shook his head. 'I don't see why I should carry the can for what they've been doing. I ain't done a thing wrong.'

'I'll check out what you've told me,' Kennett said. 'Sit tight until I get back.'

Kennett left the office and went hot-foot to the bank. He saw Chuck Busby behind the counter, serving a short line of customers. John Busby, the banker, appeared in the doorway of his office, saw Kennett, and came over to him. He was short, fleshy and smooth-cheeked, with blue eyes and fair hair — dressed in a smart, light-blue town suit.

'What can I do for you, Lew?' he demanded.

'I need to talk to Chuck.'

'Is it important? If so then I'll relieve him.'

'Yes, it is important. I need him at the law office, and he may be quite some time.'

'Is he in trouble?'

'Send him out here and I'll talk to him.'

Busby went behind the counter, spoke to his son, and Chuck threw a quick look at Kennett before coming to join him. He was a replica of his father, except that he was lean and in his early twenties.

'What's on your mind, Lew?' Busby spoke lightly, a smile on his face, but Kennett noted that his pale eyes had a shadow of fear in them.

'I'd like you to come along to the law office, Chuck. It's to do with a Reid's .32 pocket gun stolen from Overman's store. Joe Allen had it in his possession, and he said you gave it to him. I need to check out that story.'

Busby's face paled and he became tense. 'Allen is lying,' he said firmly.

'We'll go into details at the jail. Are you carrying a gun?'

'I have a .22 calibre in my right-hand pocket.'

'Stand still while I take it.' Kennett relieved Busby of the weapon. 'OK, let's get moving.'

They left the bank. Busby led the way along the sidewalk to the law office. Once inside, Kennett searched Busby, and then pointed to the chair in front of the desk.

'Sit down. What's your story?' he demanded.

'Are you gonna take my word or Allen's?' Busby demanded. He sat down heavily.

'I won't take anyone's word. I'm looking for proof, so start talking, and tell the truth. I will get the story of what really happened, so you can save time by speaking up now.'

'Allen is lying,' Busby repeated. 'Anything he tells you will be to cover up his own crookedness.'

Kennett settled himself for a long session of questions and answers, but at that moment the street door was flung open and Ossie Noble, the undertaker, came into the office.

'I was on my way to see you, Lew,' he said excitedly, 'when I saw a horse coming into town. Its rider is hung over the saddle, and there's blood on him.'

Kennett jumped up, ran to the door, and went out to the sidewalk. He saw a horse coming along the street at a canter, its rider lolling in the saddle. Kennett ran to intercept the animal, and was shocked when he recognized Lin Cooper.

10

Kennett grabbed the reins of the horse and halted it. Cooper lost his balance and fell from the saddle but Kennett caught him and lowered him to the ground. Cooper was barely conscious. His shirt front was saturated with blood. He was breathing heavily. His eyelids flickered and his eyes opened fully when he heard Kennett's voice. He reached up with his right hand and clutched Kennett's right sleeve.

'I caught up with them sidewinders,' he whispered huskily. A dribble of blood showed at a corner of his mouth. 'They laid for me but they were second best. I killed Swig Rafferty and one of Hamner's hard cases. Then Hamner got lucky and drilled me. He reckoned I was dead, and I heard him tell the others with him that they had to get to Circle B because the rest of Ivy's gang

230

was meeting up with them there. Do you know that Hamner is one of Hap Ivy's gang? He went to Circle B to take it over for Ivy. When he rode off I climbed back in my saddle and came for you.'

Cooper fell back, his strength gone. He trembled and relaxed in death, and his last breath escaped him in a long sigh. Kennett massaged his left forearm, which was hurting intolerably, and gazed down at Cooper's dead face, considering the man's last words. Then Fallon's message at the hotel flared to prominence in his mind. Sarah was riding out to Circle B!

He sprang up and ran into the office. Eke was standing guard over the still-seated Chuck Busby.

'Lock Busby in a cell until I get back, Tom,' he directed. 'I'm heading for Circle B. Round up some posse men and send them out after me. I may need gun help at the ranch.'

He turned and hastened outside, untied his horse and swung into the saddle. He spurred the animal along the street, riding as if pursued by the Devil as he recalled Sarah's words about Bull Hamner. Threats had been made against her by the big man, and by some twist of a malignant fate, she was riding straight into Hamner's clutches.

He pushed on fast, hoping he could catch Sarah before she reached the ranch. If Hamner got his hands on her he would be in a good position to get at Jake Blundell. He tried to ease his left arm into a more comfortable position to relieve the pain flaring through the limb. The jolting of the saddle was intolerable, sending spasms of agony through his wound, but he gritted his teeth and kept the horse travelling at its fastest pace. He was about ten miles from Circle B, and gazed ahead, hoping to see Sarah in the distance.

He covered five miles without incident, and then, topping a rise, saw Sarah riding steadily up an incline some two hundred yards ahead. He pulled his gun and fired a shot skywards. Sarah jerked in shock and twisted in her saddle. She recognized him and stopped her horse. He galloped up to where she was waiting and pulled his mount into a slithering, dust-raising halt.

'What's wrong?' Sarah demanded, and her face paled when he explained.

'I did tell you to remain at the hotel,' he reproved gently. 'There are some real bad men in the county, and no one will be safe until they've been dealt with; especially you and Jake.'

'I needed some clothes from the ranch,' she said. 'I didn't expect to meet trouble on a trip like this.'

'There's gonna be nothing but trouble until these hard cases are nailed down tight,' he said sharply. 'You'd better ride back to town now. I'll go on to the ranch and see what's doing. Tell me what you need and I'll bring it back to town for you.'

'If there are bad men at the ranch then you shouldn't ride in there alone.'

'It's my job. But I'm expecting a posse to follow me from town, and if there is any shooting to be done then I'll wait around for it to arrive.'

'I don't believe you. I know you, Lew. Come with me back to town.'

'Not in a hundred years. Get moving, Sarah, and I'll see you later. You're wasting my time now, and I've got things to do.'

'You look like you've done more than your share,' she observed. 'I can see your arm is giving you a lot of trouble. I'll bet Doc Mitchell told you to rest up, but you can't take advice from anyone. What you should do is send to Fairfax for help.'

'That would be a waste of time.' He shrugged. 'The sheriff would send a message back telling me to get on and do what I'm paid for.'

Sarah shook her head, tugged on her reins, and turned the horse in the direction of the distant town.

'Hold on a minute,' Kennett said. 'On second thoughts, I'd better ride with you. I can always come back for the bad men, but I'd never forgive myself if anything happened to you.'

'Come on, then.' Sarah smiled as if she had won a small victory, and set her heels against the flanks of her horse. Kennett turned his mount, but caught a flicker of movement out of the corner of his eye and glanced at the crest above. Three riders were crossing the skyline, and even as he checked them out he saw one of them draw a pistol. He spurred his horse and it jumped forward, almost colliding with Sarah's mount.

'Make a run for it,' he cried. 'We've got company!'

A Colt crashed and a slug whined over their heads. Echoes marred the silence and drifted away. Kennett winced in pain as he took his reins in his left hand and drew his pistol. Sarah went galloping away in the direction of Black Horse Creek. He turned his horse back to face the trio that had appeared, and started shooting as all three bought into the fight.

His first shot struck the man on the

left, who jerked on his reins and pulled his horse back off the crest. The other two hunched in their saddles to lessen their target area and triggered their guns, their horses stamping nervously on the crest. Slugs crackled past Kennett's head, and several struck the ground about him, raising dust spots. He felt vulnerable in the open. But the men were easing back beyond the crest. As he sent his horse to the left, looking for cover, the animal squealed and jerked, then staggered. It went on for a couple of strides before its forelegs suddenly lost strength and it went down quickly, driving its nose into the sun-baked earth.

Kennett kicked his feet clear of his stirrups and threw himself to his right as the horse fell on its left side. He hit the ground hard on his right shoulder and lost his grip on the pistol. His left arm struck the ground hard and he gasped at the flaring agony that started up. He jumped to his feet, grabbed up his pistol, and went at a run for the nearest cover: a jumble of rocks at the foot of the incline. Slugs hammered about him as he ducked into cover and lay gasping for breath.

The shooting continued for interminable moments, although he was not visible to his attackers. He lay on his belly, gripping his pistol, waiting for the storm of lead to cease. When the shooting stopped, he eased around a rock and levelled his gun. One of his attackers was halfway down the slope, riding recklessly, gun in hand and ready to shoot. Kennett swung his pistol and fired, keeping the weapon moving. His foresight came up from behind his target, passed it, and went on, moving steadily. He fired two quick shots when his sights were lined up and slightly ahead of the man, and the attacker pitched sideways out of his saddle to lie dead on the hard ground.

A rifle on the crest opened fire again and Kennett ducked. Sweat was running down his face. He grimaced at the pain in his left arm and eased to the opposite side of the rock behind which he was sheltering. A bullet struck the ground inches in front of him, showering him with dirt and shards of rock. He ducked, and stayed down until the shooting ceased. Sweat was pouring down his face.

He heard a voice yelling from the crest and peered cautiously from his cover. Two heads were showing above the skyline and he tossed slugs at them. Both men ducked hastily. Kennett dropped flat and reloaded his smoking pistol. He slid out from behind his cover and started up the slope, taking advantage of the rocks strewn on the incline. A rider pushed his mount forward on the crest and fanned his Colt .45, sending a stream of lead at Kennett, who dropped flat, crawled to his left, and eased forward to return fire. The rider moved back out of view. Kennett surged to his feet and continued up the slope, favouring his arm, determined to finish this fight without further delay.

He gained the ridge and looked around, gun ready. A rider was galloping away in the direction of the distant Circle B, and a man was lying on the ground nearby, the victim of Kennett's first shot. A horse was standing close by, its reins trailing. Kennett went to the animal, gathered up the reins and climbed into the saddle. He set out after the fleeing rider.

He was about five miles from Circle B, and aware that his trouble would not be over until he had confronted Bull Hamner and the bad men with him. He was hot and sweating. His left arm ached abominably. He pushed the horse along, but could make no impression on the rider ahead. He was filled with anger and past wondering who was doing what in this situation. He would take events as they came. He watched his surroundings as he pushed on to Circle B, hoping his posse was on its way out from town to join him.

When the buildings of the ranch

appeared ahead he rode to one side of the trail and closed in furtively, finally dismounting in a stand of timber overlooking the yard. He left the horse tethered out of sight, reloaded his pistol, and drew a Winchester out of the saddle boot. His arm hurt when he operated the rifle, but he took it along and moved into a position from which to observe the ranch.

Bull Hamner was standing on the porch of the house and the man Kennett had followed was in the act of dismounting in the yard. Three other men were standing around the front of the house, evidently waiting for something to happen. Kennett recognized two of them as having been with Hamner at the cabin in town when he had called to tell Forster's widow that her husband was dead. The other two were strangers, travel-stained and heavily armed. All the men were holding rifles. They looked as if they were awaiting orders to ride out on some illegal caper.

There was no sign of the regular

ranch crew. Kennett looked at the corral, and saw no more than half a dozen horses penned inside. Hamner looked as if he owned the place, and Kennett curbed the impulse to put a slug through the big man. The odds were too great for him to ride in and tackle them alone. He eased into deeper cover and then went back until he could watch the trail from town. He badly needed a posse.

When he spotted two riders coming at a canter along the trail from town, Kennett stiffened and shaded his eyes against the glare of the sun. Disbelief filled him when he recognized Sarah, and he gazed at her, shaking his head. What was she doing coming here instead of high-tailing it to town? He studied the man with her, and his teeth clicked together when he saw a drawn gun in the man's right hand. He was a stranger, rough-looking, and Kennett sprang to his feet and ran for the tethered horse. Sarah was a prisoner, and being taken to Hamner.

He untied the horse and swung into the saddle, ignoring the pain in his arm. He set off quickly, intending to confront the riders before they got within sight of the ranch, and he was rapidly approaching them when he saw movement off to his left and spotted two riders coming from the ranch.

Kennett cursed under his breath and quickly transferred his reins to his left hand. He drew his pistol and sent the horse into a gallop, angling to reach Sarah and her captor before the newcomers could get within range. Sarah, nearest to him, turned her head and saw him. He waved his gun at her, signalling that she should drop back out of the line of fire. The man with her had spotted the riders coming from the ranch, and was temporarily distracted. He was surprised when Sarah hauled on her reins and whirled her horse away from him. He shouted, and tried to grasp her reins but missed.

As Sarah moved away, the man raised his pistol as if to shoot her. Kennett fired instantly, his foresight covering the man's chest. Gun smoke flared and the crash of the shot hammered away across the range, echoing in a sullen roll of thunder. The man pitched out of his saddle.

Kennett set out after Sarah, angling to his right, but he was watching the two newcomers coming from the ranch. Both drew guns and started shooting. They spurred into a gallop to give chase. Sarah was high-tailing it along the trail, again heading for town. Kennett swung to his left to place himself between her and their pursuers. He fired at the two men, forcing them to separate, but still they came on fast, determined to fight.

Slugs whined around Kennett, but he was determined to save Sarah whatever the cost. He fell in behind her, twisted in his saddle, and opened a steady fire on the pursuers. Two shots later, one of the men fell off his horse. The other wheeled away and sought cover. A moment after he had disappeared from view he began to use a rifle, and the flat crack of the Winchester warned Kennett that he was in bad trouble.

Sarah was disappearing over a crest just ahead, and Kennett had a nasty sensation between his shoulder blades as he covered the last yards to safety. He was on the skyline with a prayer of relief forming in his mind when he was hit by a 44.40 slug. It was like being struck by lightning. He felt a flashing pain in his back. A black wave sprang up from inside him and he experienced a sense of flying through the air. Then, mercifully, all sensation faded and darkness enveloped him as he lost consciousness.

★　★　★

Returning to his senses was like being reborn. His eyes flickered open and he realized that he was lying on his back on thick grass. The brilliant sky was above him. Sarah was close, bending over him, her face strained and fearful, eyes filled with concern. He could hear her saying his name over and over again, but her voice was distorted. His senses were swimming. He felt no pain, was reluctant to move. His mind was blank and he had no idea where he was and what he was supposed to be doing.

A man suddenly appeared behind Sarah, gun in hand. His movement cut through the fog in Kennett's brain and his hearing returned to normal. He heard Sarah's voice calling his name. Pain returned to him like a flash flood rushing through a dry wash.

'Is he dead?' demanded the man.

Kennett disliked the question and anger seeped into his mind, chasing out some of the pain. His right hand scrabbled in the grass, trying to locate his missing pistol. He tried to sit up but felt that he was pinned to the ground by a stake driven through his chest.

'Keep still, Lew,' Sarah said, her voice sounding very loud in the surrounding silence. 'You've been shot in the back. I must get you to the ranch quickly.'

'I'll be OK,' he mumbled. 'I've got a job to do.'

'You're finished,' the man rapped. Kennett recognized him as one of the men who had been pursuing them. 'I got orders from Hamner to kill you on sight.'

He lifted his pistol to aim at Kennett, who could only gaze at his would-be executioner. But Sarah uttered a cry and lifted a pistol from the grass at her side. Kennett watched stolidly as she pointed the weapon at the man and fired. He disappeared from Kennett's view and the crash of the shot bludgeoned the silence. Kennett's mind protested at the noise. He made an effort to move and seemed to break through an invisible wall of shock, to discover that he was able to think clearly once more.

'Lie still,' Sarah said sharply.

But Kennett had recovered from inertia. He pressed his right hand against the ground and half-rolled until he could get his weight on it. He groaned as he sat up, and his senses whirled but then steadied. He looked around. The man who had intended to kill him was lying on his back nearby; blood oozed from a bullet wound in the centre of his chest.

'Where's my gun?' Kennett demanded, and Sarah handed over the pistol she was holding.

Kennett could feel pain spreading through his back, pulsating with every heartbeat. He glanced down at his chest, looking for blood, and was relieved to see his shirt front was clear. He had not been dusted both sides! He instinctively checked his gun, and fumbled for fresh cartridges to reload empty chambers.

'Fetch a horse over and I'll get into the saddle,' he said.

Sarah got to her feet. She fetched the horse of the man she had shot, and held its reins while Kennett grasped a stirrup with his right hand and laboriously hauled himself to his feet. He looked over the back of the horse and gazed around at his surroundings. The range was deserted, but he was certain the shooting would have been heard by those men still on the ranch. Bull Hamner and two others, he told himself, and he wanted Hamner. With the big man behind bars he felt he could close the rustling problem affecting the county. He holstered the pistol.

'Take a look at my back, Sarah!' He leaned heavily on the stirrup and she moved around to examine him.

'It's not as bad as I feared,' she said with relief thick in her tone. 'You must have been twisted in the saddle when he fired at you. The slug went through the side of your arm and slanted across the large muscle under the shoulder blade. And it isn't lodged there. It's just a bad flesh wound.'

'Can you push me into the saddle?' he asked. 'I can't use my left side at all.'

He tottered around the horse to its right side, lifted his right foot to the stirrup, and pulled on the saddle-horn with his right hand. Sarah pushed and lifted him from behind and he went up into the saddle, swaying almost off balance — he always mounted from the opposite side — then settled and reached for the reins.

'I want you to stick with me from now on,' he said, 'but drop back to a safe distance and follow me.'

'What are you going to do?' she demanded.

'I want Bull Hamner, and I saw him on the ranch a few minutes ago.'

'Please, Lew, let's go back to town. You're not in a fit state to try and arrest anyone and, from what I've seen of Hamner, he won't come quietly.'

'Just do like I say,' he told her sharply.

She went for her horse. Kennett held his reins in his left hand. He was hunched in the saddle, favouring his left side. Pain was beginning to envelop him and he wanted to do what he had to do before ability deserted him. He shook the reins and the horse went forward obediently. He managed a canter, and headed for the nearby ranch.

When he was in a position to view the yard he saw Hamner standing in the doorway of the house, looking as if he owned the place. Sarah came up alongside Kennett, and she was angry.

'Look at him!' she exclaimed. 'He told me once that he would own this ranch one day and I laughed at him. But there he is; standing at the door as if he had every right to be there. I want him out of here, Lew.'

'Drop back like I said, and stay there,' he replied. 'I don't need to worry about you at a time like this.'

He rode forward and entered the yard. Sarah dropped back. Kennett concentrated on the big figure standing on the porch with legs braced. Hamner's right hand was down at his side, very close to his right-hand gun. He did not move as Kennett crossed the yard. Kennett glanced around. There was no sign of other men, and he felt that this situation was all wrong. But he did not stop. He rode right up to the porch and reined in. His right hand was resting on his right thigh.

'You reckon on arresting me, huh?'

Hamner said. A leering smile stretched his lips. There was an unholy light in his narrowed eyes.

'I ain't coming quietly, Deputy. If you want me you'll have to do it the hard way.'

'I'm arresting you on suspicion of rustling,' Kennett said.

'I ain't coming quietly.' Hamner flexed the fingers of his right hand.

'What you want is of no account,' Kennett told him. 'Get your hands up or make your play. I'm taking you in — dead or alive.'

Hamner's face lost its smile and his expression showed wariness. He did not move a muscle, and yet he seemed to tense and coil his body like a well-greased spring. Kennett watched him intently, and set his hand into motion when he caught the first fraction of movement from the big man. Hamner flowed into motion and his pistol seemed to leap into his hand. Kennett reacted simultaneously, pulling his gun and cocking it as it levelled.

He squeezed his trigger a split second before Hamner did and the rustler jerked under the impact of the slug. He fell back against the front wall of the house and seemed to freeze there, eyes wide, teeth showing in a snarl of defiance. Blood spurted from the centre of his wide chest. Then the life ran out of him and he fell to the floor, kicking spasmodically as he died.

The strength ran out of Kennett then and he sagged in the saddle. He dropped his pistol and put his right hand on the saddle-horn, but it failed to take his weight and he slid sideways out of the saddle. As he hit the ground he was thinking that the trouble was over. He had enough evidence to tidy up the problems back in town, and he had shot the hell out of Hap Ivy's gang. His senses fled as he bit the dust, and when Sarah bent over him she was surprised to see a little smile of satisfaction on his taut lips.

Other titles in the
Linford Western Library:

COFFIN FOR AN OUTLAW

Thomas McNulty

When legendary lawman-turned-bounty-hunter Chance Sonnet reappears, the word spreads that he wants Eric Cabot dead. Cabot, in the dark as to Sonnet's motives, sends his men to kill Sonnet first — but the task proves more difficult than he imagines. Sonnet also finds himself pursued by a plucky newspaperwoman and an old Texas Ranger who knows something of his past. Blazing a trail in a buckboard and hauling a pine coffin intended for Cabot, Chance Sonnet is a man haunted by the past and facing a future steeped in blood.

A TOWN CALLED INNOCENCE

Simon Webb

Falsely convicted of murder and sentenced to hang, it seems as though the end of young Will Bennett's life is in sight — but a strange circumstance of fate frees him to track down the real murderer. His journey takes him to a Texas town where he learns the truth about the plot that nearly sent him to the gallows. Bennett's journey from the town called Innocence to the final showdown with the man who framed him for murder ends in a bloody shootout, from which only one man will emerge alive.

INVITATION TO A FUNERAL

Jethro Kyle

At twenty-eight, Joseph Carver is the youngest college professor in the United States. He is estranged from his father Will, the sheriff of a Kansas town. When Will is gunned down during a bank robbery and Joseph's mother dies of grief shortly thereafter, he is forced to face his family demons and return home. After his parents' funeral, he arms himself and sets off in pursuit of the men who shot his father. His quest takes him into the Indian Nations, where he receives help of a most surprising nature . . .